Edward Belcher Callender

The Leg-Pullers

Politics as she is applied - A tale of the Puritan commonwealth

Edward Belcher Callender

The Leg-Pullers
Politics as she is applied - A tale of the Puritan commonwealth

ISBN/EAN: 9783337344726

Printed in Europe, USA, Canada, Australia, Japan

Cover: Foto ©Andreas Hilbeck / pixelio.de

More available books at **www.hansebooks.com**

THE

LEG - PULLERS;

OR,

POLITICS AS SHE IS APPLIED.

A TALE OF

THE PURITAN COMMONWEALTH.

BY

ONE WHO HAS BEEN THERE.

PEMBERTON SQUARE PUBLISHING CO.

BOSTON, MASS.

CONTENTS.

CHAPTER I.

Everywhere is bustle and excitement; yet order and red tape prevail. Men are elbowing their way through the crowded corridors and up the narrow stairways. Blue-coated, brass-buttoned messengers are hurrying hither and thither, their arms filled with documents and manuals, answering inquiries, giving directions. Officers brandish their long wands and usher committees to their duties. In the galleries is the rustle of ladies' dresses; the conversation of spectators is in the hallways. Committees are announcing that they have attended to their duties and that His Excellency was pleased to learn this, and congratulated the bodies on having done that, etc., etc. The impress of some great undertaking is stamped on all things.

It is the annual Puritan farce, the assembling of the General Court of the ancient Common-wealth of Massachusetts — the hodge-podge of legalized blackmail which masquerades under the cloak of representative popular government. Here for six months will those two hundred and eighty chosen men sit, explaining

to each other what is apparent and concealing
what is obscure, and so compile a thousand-
paged volume of formal verbiage that shall
saddle every occupation, trade and employment
with destructive conditions and restrictions,
unless, forsooth, smart money be paid not to
do so. The Arab sheik exacting from the
traveller in his dominion a fee for protection
from his own robbers stands on no lower grade.
If it is true, what Napoleon said of the church,
that it was an institution designed to prevent
the poor from robbing the rich, we shall see it
is equally true that popular government is a
cunningly devised scheme whereby with im-
punity the shiftless may successfully blackmail
the thrifty.

Looking over this assembly, one's attention
is arrested by a figure of powerful frame and
intellectual countenance that belongs to one
who is far and away the lion in this menagerie.
The forehead plainly tells this man has memory
and reasoning faculties in fullest measure given.
The massive head is crowned with a halo of
coarse and wavy hair of iron gray. The full
throat and burly neck recall the sketches of
great Mirabeau. Wheresoever in that chamber he may be, he is a focus for all eyes. He
is armed at all points. Is it in debate, then
merciless his shafts of ridicule, his eloquence
a rushing torrent. Is it votes he is after, he

strides through the aisles, signalling to this
friend and that, and moulding even enemies to
his will. In all he says or does he is affirmative, sways this body, is a born leader of men.
For three years now has he dominated this
political witan; sometimes with this party has
'he been enrolled, sometimes with that, and
always on a platform of his own. None have
seen more clearly than he the purport of a well-
made plank on which to stand. He knows,
none better, that platforms are simply statements of principles which the nominee will be
willing to go back on for a consideration; they
are bait for the voter and fruit for the candidate; they are hints of just what the candidate
will not do if properly paid. Hence this man's
platform has been avowed hostility to corporate
influence. His vote the corporations have
never failed to secure, if but the proper consideration was forthcoming.

A messenger has just pushed before him for
his signature the book in which is kept the
official oath, to which he has often subscribed
and as often broken. He signs his name and
address. It reads:—

MILES MULVENNA, MILLVILLE.

Ill-dispositioned and disappointed politicians
there were, who maliciously buzzed to newly-
elected representatives that Mulvenna took

from both sides, and therefore was not to be trusted. In politics an "honest" man is one who will stay bought; an "approachable" man is one who entertains no special channel for the receipt of customs, but may be offered financial consideration by anybody. If Mulvenna was not of the first type, he certainly could claim close affinity to the second. In the case of any other individual the purity press would have made it matter of serious comment; for some unknown reason Mulvenna was never assailed. Perhaps his depredations were on too large a scale. Great robbers excite only admiration, they suffer punishment never.

Many years before the opening of our story, the Millville *Democrat* had charged venality in the public conduct of Mulvenna, but this did not injure Mulvenna in the estimation of those who comprised his constituency. Even the wealthier and more respectable of Millville citizens, whom one would suppose might be shocked at the disclosures of the Millville *Democrat*, saw in them only an argument in Mulvenna's favor. "If these corporations," said one, "come to our selectmen with their nefarious schemes to make millions, why should not Mulvenna get his dollar out of them if he is cunning enough to do it"? Society in general took the same view. "Ability," says the philosopher, "relieves the black-

ness of corruption with a fringe of light."
History, that is, what we call history, is in line
with this teaching. Crime is transitory,
ephemeral; but ability, that is lasting.

The only effect of the attack of the Millville
Democrat was to enlarge Mulvenna's vote for
whatever office he might be a candidate. In
Massachusetts one has but to point out with
absolute proof the wretched venality of a public
servant, and such servant at once becomes a
martyr, and perpetual power is granted him.
Mulvenna pocketed the wages of corruption,
asked the blessing of Almighty God on the in-
vestment, and He had answered the prayer by
increased majorities. So Mulvenna had made
full proof of his calling. He could now sell
himself to any one for any price, and his supporters would only applaud the more.

Still, Mulvenna understood human nature ;
he rightly estimated the force of public opinion,
which is simply crystalized envy. The profits
of politics must never appear, else there be
excited jealousy in the minds of the covetous,
who might then seek the office. His constant
care, therefore, was to conceal all manifestation
of his wealth. He was fully cognizant of the
fact that the world judges the extent of a man's
purse not by what he saves and hides, but by
what he spends and displays. So Mulvenna
restrained his natural desire to live freely and

entertain lavishly.   He occupied the same
dwelling year after year, wore the same clothes,
indulged in no pleasures which cost him anything.   If it became necessary to "treat the
bhoys," as it is called, he supplied small beer,
when others would have felt called upon to
open wine.   If other politicians distributed
cigars to their constituents, he limited his
tobacco largesses to plug, and offered that.   If
he invested his constantly-increasing gains,
they were invested elsewhere than in Millville.
There he owned neither lands nor heredita-
ments; the very house he lived in was hired.
He had no visible means of support, so he
brought his actual living expenses within the
limits of his legislative salary.   Soon the old
scandal of the Millville *Democrat* was forgotten.
People said: "If Mulvenna is really corrupt,
why does he not show it; where is the evidence
of his ill-gotten gains?   He has nothing; he is
poor as a rat."   This was the precise impression Mulvenna wished to create, at least in
Millville.

At the State House, Mulvenna posed as the
broad-minded friend of the wage-earner, and as
an advocate for toleration in all things.   Not
always sincere in this regard, of course.   When
some of the more rash of his race and faith
endeavored to pass legislation doing away
with Puritan customs and usages, he strongly

objected, saying to his friends, "Don't destroy
Puritanism; preserve it! It helps *us*. It gives
us the usufruct. Puritanism causes its followers to.dry up, to restrain their natural desires,
to live cheaper, eat cheaper food and gradually
grow poorer. It makes a man miss-see the
real gain to be derived from existence. Look
around you! See what fools these Yankee
Puritans are! They are always wanting to put
some restriction on this or that trade, limit the
capital of corporations, prevent their consolidation, while we get pay by removing these very
shackles from the limbs of fettered industries.
Cannot you see? *We* are really using *them*.
They shake the tree and *we* gather the fruit;
while *they* starve, *we* garner the shekels. Therefore don't suppress Puritanism. Spread it!
Spread it! It's the source of *our* gain." Mulvenna clearly saw that Puritanism paralyzes the
man; the glamour which it pretended to throw
about life had resulted in destroying the beauty
of Sunday, had put a damper on the glorious
inspirations of genius and checked the noble
ambitions of mankind. For Puritanism builds
no grand churches; paints no great works of
art; writes no great poems; sings no grand
songs; in fine, does nothing human and admirable—while its great fad of popular government is simply a covering for a grosser tyranny
than has.yet existed among men, to wit, black-

mail. Such a system must finally petrify the believer in it. The more its principles could be adopted by the opposition the better, the surer the final elimination of that opposition. So when the Puritan customs and ideas were attacked, Mulvenna came to their rescue. They had no more eloquent champion on the floor of the house. He knew it increased the harvest for him.

In Millville he was the well-beloved father of the people. His experiences had given him a smattering of law and its practices. The poor who could not pay an attorney's fee, consulted him freely, without money and without price. He drew their mortgages, assignments of earnings, bills of sale and what not, refusing in all instances the least reward, except that which comes at the caucus and the ballot box. There he expected full measure. Were the wages of an operative trusteed, he attended to the settlement thereof. If, occasionally, a wage-earning constituent was before the criminal court, Mulvenna's influence with district attorney and with judge was sought and freely given. Therefore the more would the ordinary voters insist that Mulvenna could not be corrupt. He had even refused *their* pay on matters of business wholly outside of political duty. Well, others before him had refused a crown, and yet had been ambitious. But at the State House, far removed from Millville, it was far different. There, nothing was allowed to pass him by without its doit. If before a debate some agent interested in a pending bill had omitted to make satisfactory arrangements with Mulvenna, he with plausible words suggested to the House that there might be merit in the bill, but still he needed time for further examination, and so would move its further consideration to some other day. When Mulvenna did this, all knew what it meant. The captious said: "Miles has not been seen." Others winked, and quietly suggested: "Ah, Mulvenna signals for stuff"! Nothing that could pay tribute was allowed to escape; and the settlements never carried thirty days' credit, either. In fact, a little closet, leading out of a narrow corridor, where Mulvenna made his trades and adjusted the daily balances with the various agents, was (and is to this day) familiarly known as "Mulvenna's Exchange." Politics with him was pure, simple business (as with whom is it not!'); only he was more extortionate in his demands, and more exacting as to payment,—in other words, a better business man.

To return, Mulvenna had signed the oath, and now was ready for business. Always industrious, a great economizer of time, even thus early in the session was he laying his plans of attack. He draws from his pocket a

paper containing the list of the various matters
of proposed legislation, which, as required by
law, had been duly advertised. Representatives
generally supposed that this provision of law
was necessary in order to prevent soulless corporations from springing unholy legislation on
the people; as a matter of fact, it was primarily
designed to afford the like of Mulvenna early
intimation as to where to strike for business.
"Ah," he mused, as he eagerly scanned the
paper: "Petition of Roger Rosenthal, *et al.*
for an act to incorporate the Twenty Land
Associates. Rosenthal, Rosenthal, let me see,
that must be the rich brewer. There ought
to be vest and trousers in that." He put a
dot side of the printed title. "Petition for an
act dividing the town of Boxford, that ought
to cut up fat." Another dot, with unintelligible
sign near it. " Petition to increase the capital
stock of the Franklin and Berkshire Railroad,
well, well, there ought to be enough in that to
pay Dick's tuition at Harvard next year." Dick
was Mulvenna's only child, his joy and pride;
the great desire of Mulvenna's life was to see
his son a judge. And now the eyes brighten
and a smile of cupidity plays about the mouth
as he reads, " Petition of the various water
companies within twenty miles of Boston for
power to increase their several capital stocks
and to provide for gradual consolidation in a

new corporation without limit of capital." The
climax had been reached! Surely in such a
matter as this last there would be a five-story
tenement house! "I guess I better take an
early look at that petition. I wonder who the
attorney is in that case. I hope it is not Gentry,
d——n him"! Gentry had the reputation of
cutting down on his agreements, and Miles
knew in such cases it was safer to deal with the
principals.

The house adjourned early, and as the
Speaker entered his private room he was
accompanied by a flashily-dressed gentleman
with whom he appeared to be on terms of great
intimacy.

"Who is that"? asked Mulvenna of the obsequious and oleaginous doorkeeper.

"That! don't *you* know? Why, that's the
president of the new Metropolitan Water Supply Company; that's going to be the biggest
piece of legislation this year, you want to be
in it."

"Well, let me alone; don't you fear, I'll
connect! What's his name"?

"Justin Bulrush Morgan."

"What's his business here"?

"Arranging with the Speaker about the com-
position of the water committee."

"My game," thought Mulvenna, "what luck"!

"Here," he whispered, "when he leaves the

room let me know at once; I'll be down in the rotunda."

No one dared to disobey Mulvenna. He did wait in the rotunda. He did see the water magnate, who much annoyed and against his will, finally agreed to receive Mr. Mulvenna the next day at the office of the company, and what transpired at that interview can be imagined from the description Mr. Morgan gave of it at a dinner company a few days later.

CHAPTER II.

ETHICS OF CORRUPTION.

"Good afternoon, Mr. Gentry." The words were uttered by a smiling and eupeptic individual, who stood in a cringing attitude before the person to whom they were addressed, although, considering the physical appearance of the two men, one would have supposed that Gentry should have humbled himself to the new comer. "You've sent for me and I am here," went on the smiling individual, who was distinguished in his daily contact with the world by his extreme affability, though in trials of accident causes, the sorrow and sympathy he always expressed for his unfortunate clients had earned for him the sobriquet of the "Niobe of the Bar"—all tears. Small, compact, hatchet-faced Gentry turned nervously, motioned to a large leathern-covered chair in the private office of "Gentry, Attorney," and said: "Pray, be seated." Gentry buttoned up his four-buttoned cutaway, closed the door communicating with the outer office, scowled a trifle to collect his faculties, assumed a direct and impressive air, and prefacing his remarks with a cough and two or three "ahs," went on as follows:

"I have sent for you, Mr. Denning, because, as counsel for the Metropolitan Water Supply Company, I have a matter coming before the present legislature in which I may need your assistance. You will understand that I do not do this as a matter of friendship at all, but because I need you. I cannot stand those fellows on the hill, and all their tricks. I lose my temper in talking with them; while I am impressed with the facts that your "*suaviter in modo*" might materially help my clients, where my "*graviter in re*" would prove detrimental. I shall want you to present our case before the joint committee of the House and Senate."

Mr. Denning, sanguine, smiling and rotund, completely filling the chair in which he was comfortably seated, nodded his assent. He made no reply unless it was contained in his eternal and insufferably obsequious smile.

"Well," said Gentry deprecatingly, "I suppose you feel a retainer should be forthcoming"? Denning beamed again. Pulling down his check book, the consulting counsel of the Metropolitan Water Supply Company took up his pen and casually remarked:

"I suppose a thousand will be satisfactory"?

A smile and an audible "perfectly" was the answer, and the conversation went on in about this fashion: —

Gentry: — "Now, what do you know about

the present legislature? Do you suppose we have got to be soaked by Mulvenna"?

Denning (smiling):—" Possibly we can find some way to prevent it."

Gentry:—" It's rather a hungry body, I am told."

Denning (still smiling):—" That is the general impression."

Gentry:—"Well, notwithstanding your platitudes of 'the public morality and rugged virtue of the Massachusetts hill towns' that you have been giving the 'hayseeds' at the annual cattle fairs, I still take it you can find some way to corral their cupidity"?

Denning (smiling as ever):—"There are few attorneys at the Bar so accurate in their judgment as you have the reputation of being."

Gentry:—" What do you say is the first thing to do, in a case of this magnitude? We must proceed carefully, and make no mistakes, especially at the beginning."

Denning (after a moment's thought, the smile never leaving his face):—" Brother Gentry, do you know Ormond"?

Gentry:—" What, ' Pop'"?

Denning (smiling):—" Yes, but your tone is disparaging."

Gentry:—"Well, he has not a very large practice, has he—been sort of unfortunate in extending his clientage"?

Denning : — " Bright men sometimes are. I tell you, Ormond knows the real bottom of everything — he is omnivorous.   From the Police Court to the Senate, he is master of every sort of practice and detail.   I think we better have a talk with him."

Gentry : — " Nonsense, I have never seen any great display of ability on his part. He does not have a half dozen cases before the full bench in any one year. What possible good can he be to us? Of course the more people I have to hire the less there is in it for me."

Denning : — " What good can he be to us! Why he can do more on the hill in the way of votes — and it is votes you want — than both of us, craving your pardon " (obsequious smile), " can do together. Let's have a session with him at any rate."

Gentry : — " I suppose a retainer of fifty dollars would set him going, would n't it "?

Denning (for once he did not smile): — " Brother Gentry, I would not insult him by offering less than double that amount.   I tell you this man is a genius, as a vote getter, at any rate."

Gentry : — " You are liberal with other people's money."

" Denning (the smile returning): — " My dear Mr. Gentry, let us be fair in everything. With a retainer of goodly proportion in my own pocket, I could not look 'Pop' in the face and ask his advice unless I offered him a fair return."

Gentry:—"O! Don't understand that I wish to be mean in this matter. Let's see, his office is only a few doors below. No time like the present. We'll be off and see your Mr. Know-it-all" (this last with contempt).

The two attorneys marched out of the office and proceeded, with the dignity befitting so important a case, down the street to the building where Mr. Ormond's office was located, and taking the elevator were rapidly whisked up to the top floor.

"*Sic itur ad astra*, I suppose you think," said Gentry with a grin.

"Well, when you return to your quarters it will be a case of *facile descensus averni*, replied Denning, smiling. Gentry scowled. They opened the door and entered the law office of Richard Ormond, Esq., familiarly known as "Pop."

"Brother Ormond," began Gentry, perhaps you could be of service to Brother Denning and myself."

The tone was harsh, grating and disagreeable.

"I have a matter before the General Court, and as I understand it you have a remarkably effective influence with many of the members, derived, I have no doubt, from the fact that you are generally credited with dividing your fees with them."

"Something no one ever accused you of doing, Mr. Gentry."

"There, now, don't be severe, I meant no offense. Still (trying to be jocose and easy), it is true, is n't it"?

"If it were true, it would be doing nothing more than the Saviour's behest, 'to feed His lambs,' would it"?

"Your knowledge extends even to the scriptures, then"?

Ormond bowed stiffly. Denning was ill at ease. The manner in which Gentry had addressed Ormond nettled him. He gently put his hand on Ormond's shoulder, smiled, of course, and whispered, "Can we see you alone"?

They had been standing in the outer office, a large square room, with windows commanding a superb view of the harbor. The clerks, students, and typewriter occupied desks in this room. The office adjoining this was apparently a consulting room, while beyond, leading out from the latter, was a long rambling room, a combination of library, sitting-room and growlery. It was somewhat different from any ordinary appendage to a lawyer's office. Bookcases lined the sides of the room. In the shelves on one side might be found the English reports from Plowden and Pere William to the date hereof; at the further end of the room a large old-fashioned open fireplace held two smouldering logs of hickory and oak. Extending from the mantel nearly to the ceiling were shelves filled with volumes of legislative documents and House and Senate journals. On the other side of the room, books of general literature, poetry, history and philosophy were jumbled together in endless confusion. Theophrastus and Lander, Plato and Montaigne, Æschylus and Shakspeare, Homer and Robert Burns. Above the books, a few rare prints. Over the door was an engraving of Belisarious in a broad oak frame, into which had been burnt the lines of Longfellow, from the poem of that name: —

Ah! vainest of all things
Is the gratitude of kings.
The plaudits of the crowd
Are but the clatter of feet
At midnight in the street,
Hollow and restless and loud.

The windows were draped with curtains of a Turkey red, such as one might often see in a collegian's chamber, the window seats themselves had cushions of soft, tan-colored leather. A number of huge old-fashioned arm-chairs were scattered around the room, one stiff-backed wooden chair was placed close to the broad oaken table, piled high with papers and with

books.   A comfortable lounge was placed
cross-ways at the end of the room.   This was
the " den " of one who was scholar, *littérateur*
and politician,—Jack of all trades, perhaps, if he
was not master of one,—as Denning had said,
omnivorous.

" Suppose we go in here," said Ormond, lead-
.ing the way into his sanctum.

" What a wonderful view you have from your
windows," remarked Denning, as he gazed down
the harbor.

" Yes, yes, I have to see the water; my stars
would not let me live if I did not get a daily
glimpse of the ocean."

" A yachtsman "? queried Gentry.

"No, I have not been on the water these ten
years, but I must see it, I must be near it.   It
is life to me."

Whether Ormond had ever followed the sea
for a livelihood no one knew.   He never said
he had, but it was generally observable in his
conversation that he employed nautical phrases
in his metaphors and drew his similes from the
historic shores of the Mediterranean.   Ormond, or as he will be hereafter called, " Pop,"
for everybody called him Pop, seated himself
in the stiff-backed chair, while his visitors
rested lazily in the large arm-chairs.   Pop
looked at his callers enquiringly for a while,
when Gentry broke the silence, laying a hun-

dred-dollar bill upon the table and pushing it towards Pop with, "I (it was always 'I' with Gentry) have come to retain you in a matter of 'mine' before the legislature, where 'I' may have occasion to consult you as regards the best method of procedure."

"You're very kind. You want to know how to point the ship. Well, if I can answer, pray go ahead and ask me what you want to know."

Gentry had handed Pop a copy of the petition for the consolidation of the various water companies referred to in the first chapter. Reading it carefully, Pop looked up and asked if it had been properly advertised, and being answered in the affirmative, remarked: —

"There is no need of a suspension of the rules in order to refer it to a committee. We shall not have that to trouble us. Have you decided to what committee it shall be referred"?

"I suppose Mercantile Affairs; it relates to incorporation."

" That's a boodle committee, you know, and most of its members come from this vicinity, where very definite ideas exist about the reciprocal relations of corporations and legislators. Why should it not go to Water Supply, that's a better committee for you"?

"Mr. Morgan, president of the new company, was advised to have it referred to Mercantile Affairs."

Pop shook his head. "It's to be a boodle year, anyhow, and that's an extravagant committee."

"But it contains a number of the Speaker's friends, and he has intimated he wishes it to go to them."

"That settles it; we need the Speaker on our side, and he, of course, wants his friends well looked after. Mercantile Affairs is generally the Speaker's pet."

"What hostile interests will be used as a pretext for opposition to the bill"?

"The usual cry against excessive capitalization, raised by several water meter companies who have patent processes they wish us to adopt."

"Then of course you will want the bill reported in the House, and in the meantime they will buy the Senate and try to beat you there. Now the first thing to do is to put all your lines at work on the Senate."

"Before the bill is reported from the Committee"?

"Unquestionably. Committee hearings are mere bluffs to satisfy the outside world. It does not matter which side is the more ably presented, the committee will decide as it is fixed. That is an easy matter with a committee prepared under the shaping hand of the speaker. The great danger is the adverse vote of the Senate after the bill has passed the House. If you delay putting your work in there now, you may find yourself in a position where you will be sailing pretty close to the wind. Secure your Senate now. Next you must be sure of your Governor."

"Well, I contributed pretty heavily to his campaign; so did Denning, here, while Morgan, it is generally understood, was the largest single contributor on the list. The Governor will hardly dare to veto any bill that we send him."

"It's not the veto I fear; it's his desire not to either sign or veto. He might prevent its coming to him at all. His Excellency is ambitious, wants to be United States Senator, would like to please all, would not wish to veto your bill and thus lose the great financial backing he might otherwise have; and at the same time would be equally disinclined to sign a bill against which the wage-earners would cry out as hostile to the interests of the people. Nothing can be easier than for some of his staff to indicate to this or that Senator that the Governor does not want the bill to come to him, and so it will be smothered in the Senate. You never knew a staff officer that was not tickled to death to be instructed to meddle in the legislative affairs of the government, and fancy himself an important personage. Be sure of your Governor." Pop was looking intently at Gentry. Gentry listened, somewhat against his will. He could not meet the steady, seer-like gaze of those peering blue eyes, which seemed to fathom his inmost mind. He disliked to have any attorney appear to advise him. Finally he inquired: "Have you any idea when we can have the case heard by the committee"?

"That," said Pop, "is the point I am coming to. My judgment is that you cannot do it too quickly. I take it for granted you will have your committee well in hand"? Gentry bowed.

"This is a matter of great interest, a big job, and your bill, in order to go through easily, must be considered either at the very beginning or very end of the session. The first of the session, if you handle your matter rightly, is the better for success."

"Why"?

"Perfectly plain. At that time the new members have not become acquainted with each other, or with the channels through which they can make their claims for compensation. As yet they are all at sea. The older members will not dare so early to stir up their new associates with the desire of gain. A few good speakers on the floor can swing the day for you. So retain the best talkers at once. By early consideration you escape heavy black-mail."

"Now," continued Pop, "how about the papers? This is important only in view of having them keep their mouths shut; their advocacy is of little avail, besides, it stirs things up and draws attention to the measure, so that the legislators will wonder if there may not be some stuff in it."

"I think, Mr. Ormond, my clients have standing enough in the community to be on the right side of the editors."

"There, you are going out of your course again. I do not refer to the editorials. I mean the reporters, the fourth estate. It makes a vast difference whether these watchful gentlemen in the gallery insert a suggestion here, or a slur there, intimating corruption, the putting through of a 'job' or the existence of log rolling. A reporter's good-will is worth more than a column of editorials. As I intimated before, you must have the good talkers with you, if the debate on your bill is early in the session. At the end of the session they are not needed, the votes can be got some other way. Again, at the beginning of a session you do not need much of a lobby, for a lobby is not of much value then, not having become acquainted with the new members. Not that I decry the lobby. It's a very valuable organization in its way, has an immense fund of information regarding the representatives of the people, knows their special weaknesses, has the acquaintance of their chief supporters. It's not at all the despicable thing the purity press would have one believe. In truth the 'third house' contains more brains than the other two, and it's a question if it does not surpass them in honesty. For I fancy in the last analysis it will be found that the lobby stands as a bulwark to ward off the blackmailer from his victim. Speaking of the lobby, I see the Senate is trying to prevent its operating this year. This simply bears out what I said, that this is a boodle legislature. It wants to do its own lobbying, collar the "stuff," as it is called, and receive an extra commission for handling the money. Speaking of the talkers, have you Mulvenna with you"?

"Morgan will attend to that. He has already had one interview with him."

Gentry had been worrying about the attitude of Mulvenna toward the bill, when he and Denning were discussing matters earlier in the afternoon. But, as Pop unrolled his plans, he made up his mind that he might want Mulvenna to oppose the bill, so that it might not slip through too easily. Gentry had the reputation among insiders in the "lobby" of continually putting his clients into trouble for the purpose of extricating them therefrom, and thereby earning a larger fee. Gentry, in his own mind, proposed to handle Mulvenna himself. Admitting the correctness of Pop's advice as to proceeding in the early part of the session, he was scheming also to make it as difficult as possible for his clients to get the bill through. The more labor on Gentry's part, the greater his fee. As he thought of his schemes, he could not avoid the searching glance of Pop's seer-like eyes. He felt intuitively that his desire for double-dealing was observed and known to Pop, and he would escape his gaze.

"There is also another advantage," went on Pop, "in early consideration. You will not be obliged to hire the 'gravel train.' That is quite an item. It takes some weeks to organize and equip, so you need not fear any 'hollering' from that source; but you would certainly have to expect it later in the session. And the 'gravel train' this year promises to be very long and difficult to handle."

"That is all very well, Pop," said Denning, noticing Gentry's restiveness, "but your ideas of this noble trust of self-government is somewhat different from that given in the books."

"Likely enough; but it is well to look at things as they are. Why, my dear sir, a hundred years ago, Volney told us, truly, that the science of government was to 'oppress prudently.' We have substituted popular government for the monarchy, but we cannot alter life. The tyrant is changed, the tyranny remains the same. If excessive taxation, military service, and debased coin were the weapons of the monarchy, blackmail is the secret instrument of the republic. Oppression exists everywhere. It always has. It always will. It exists in every department of life, only under different names—but it is always oppression, extortion, squeezing. A legislator does not change his inclination by becoming a legislator. He still oppresses, extorts; if he only 'oppresses prudently,' all is well. You have to do these things I have indicated. Your representatives and senators require it. So long as their extortion is not excessive, they are safe and you are safe." A pause. Gentry was growing nervous. Denning's smile was growing fainter. Pop was glowing with his theory.

"Besides, rich corporations know that in order to maintain their wealth they must regard the demands of the public's servants. And better service is obtainable by purchasing the servants and directing their course than to trust development and improvements to the rather inferior brains of average legislators, no matter how pure. See how easily leaders of workingmen's club or farmers' political movements are influenced; then the country editor can 'see new light' with such little effort, while the mushy intellects of the few rural clergymen who essay practical politics, can always be bought by indirect methods." Here Gentry interrupted:—

"There is a remedy for all this. Elect no man to office who is not free from debt; financial competence is one of the best securities against the disposition to blackmail. When State legislatures are composed entirely of men whose incomes habitually exceed their expenses, the problem of 'corruption,' or, as you put it, blackmail, is solved. Until then we may look for bribery, wherever water works, gas works, electrical light companies (to say nothing of granting street franchises or regulating liquor and tobacco licenses) are up for consideration."

"No! no"! chimed in Pop, "there you are wrong again. The greatest and honestest men in all history have been the poorest. Take the long list of your justly celebrated governors, from penniless Sam Adams to poor Banks, the most incorruptible in every instance have been those who were very meanly possessed of this world's goods. No, let us take things as we find them ; perhaps the existence of blackmail is a divine regulation of the Almighty—one way in which He provides that the race shall not always be to the swift, or the battle to the strong."

Gentry did not like the steadfast glance of those eyes. So, rising from his chair and remarking that it was a busy day with him, and that he would call again, and further impressing on Pop that for the present he must keep in the background as "silent counsel," the leading adviser of the Metropolitan Water Supply Company, attended by Mr. Denning, departed.

Pop stood alone in the twilight, twirled his retainer in his grasp, and wondered why Gentry had not taken it back.

What the past history of this trig, lithe, spry, keen, young-old man might be was a mystery to all. That he was a gentleman, as regards dress, at any rate, all admitted; so neat and appropriate his apparel, that what he wore was never especially noticed: the effect was satisfactory. Where he got his title of "Pop" was equally a mystery, unless it came from his interest in children, and their fondness for him. The sight of a chubby-faced infant in its baby carriage would draw him from any press of business, so he must stop and whistle to it, and listen to the music of its prattle. Had Pop ever had children of his own and lost them? None could say. Years after the date of this story, when Pop died, searching in the pockets of his waistcoat, they pulled therefrom a knit sock, that once must have protected the tiniest of little feet—pressed flat and somewhat frayed; for many years must it have been carried there, memento of the past. Once observing a nursery maid scolding her little charge for some harmless prank, he pleasantly chided her with a " Now, now, my good woman, don't scowl; never look crossly at a child. One such sour look might poison its whole after life. Children should see none but happy, sunny faces; there will be shadows enough for them by-and-by."

Tender to a fault, suffering in others always touched him, and remedy it he must. One bitter, blustering, snowy night, seeing a woman in scanty rags, huddled with her babe in a narrow doorway to escape the fury of the blast, he took from his own shoulders his newly-purchased coat, and wrapping it about the mother and the child, said nothing, but hurried on to his lodgings, shivering and chattering all the while.

The younger members of the bar, worried and troubled over their cases, could always freely seek the advice of Pop. He straightened out their pleadings for them, gave them choice hints as to the introduction and exclusion of evidence, and instructed them how best to wring the law from acrid and obtuse justices. As for his own practice, he never seemed to care. · He went from one line of employment to another with equal ease, did nothing to increase business, distributed no cards to hospital internes to assure him plethora of tort cases, employed no runners to gather in collections

for him, never lowered himself to his clients,— if
they were rascals, told them so and refused to
do their bidding,—seemed to like nothing better
than without hope of reward to right some
wrong that upstart wealth had placed upon the
defenceless. His friends and intimates were a
curious lot. Most had seen only the seamy
side of life; broken-down and breaking-up
attorneys, decayed merchants and brokers who
had failed, as they call it, in business,insolvents
and ne'er-do-wells, dissipated journalists and
hard-up actors, and many a one whose prayers
would be her only passport into Heaven. Still,
during all these years of slight financial returns,
bearing carping criticism and instanced as a
failure, Pop chipped on cheerfully through life,
merrily conquering the annoyances of each day
and trying to see where the fun of existence
might be gathered, for he knew it was laughter
and not tears that keeps well oiled the human
machine and alone makes life endurable. How
could such a man be successful, Mr. Gentry?
The office now was deserted, save for Pop.
Clerks, students and typewriter (never greatly
overworked in that office) had now gone home.
Alone, he stood musing in the deepening twilight. Slight, erect, willowy, his neatly-trimmed
white hair making a strong contrast with
the bright blue eyes and fresh pink complexion,
like a rose-bud in the snow. The figure of a

boy, the color of a girl, the locks of an old man. Had that hair turned white in one night from some sudden shock? Was he still a youth, or had remorseless age, as it stole on him, cared for him too deeply to show its traces upon cheeks and frame? None could answer. To those who knew him he was still a mystery. For us, save as he acts in this story, he will remain, at present, a mystery.

CHAPTER. III.

SCIENCE OF NUTRITION.

The advice of Pop, so far as the early consideration of the Metropolitan Water Bill was concerned, was strictly followed. Mr. Gentry, realizing the importance of things moving smoothly and swiftly before the committee, had arranged through Mr. Denning to retain one Wilkes, a gentleman intimately acquainted with legislative affairs, to learn the wishes of the committee in matters of remuneration. All preliminaries having been satisfactorily settled, and notice of the hearing duly given, at the hour appointed the full committee with smiling countenances and words of pleasant recognition to Denning, who was to present the case, and to Wilkes, who had so kindly put them in communication with the "dispensers of stuff," took their seats and called for the names of the counsel for the petitioners (already well known to them), and for those who appeared in opposition.

A somewhat seedy-looking individual announced that he represented the various labor organizations who originally were opposed to

the bill, but on the representations of the petitioners' counsel that the consolidation of the
various water companies would necessitate
great public improvements and result in the
construction of much work where labor would
be required, he felt that the proposed consolidation would be a direct benefit to the wage-
earners, and, therefore, should be favored by
the State, and in behalf of the different labor
unions which he represented, he withdrew all
opposition on their part to the proposed legislation, suggesting merely to the committee the
feasibility of inserting in the bill a clause
requiring all laborers on any work constructed
by the new company to be members of some.
duly accredited labor union. This labor agita-
tor received a regular salary for guarding the
rights of labor in all matters before the legislature. In addition, Mr. Wilkes had put into his
hands for his own emolument a crisp five hun-
dred-dollar bill as an extra inducement to
withdraw his opposition. So labor had maintained its right and Mr. Birdinan (such was his
name) had earned his salary as well as pocketed
a neat *douceur.* Labor had "oppressed prudently." "True," said Mr. Wilkes, in explaining this transaction to Mr. Denning, "true it
is blackmail on Birdinan's part, but then we
still the 'labor' cry, and that is one of the
worst slogans to introduce into a legislative

fight. Senators and representatives stand in awe of the labor vote, controlled by such chaps as · Birdinan." The committee bowed its acknowledgment of Mr. Birdinan's withdrawal.

Thereupon up rose Mr. Fearnaught of the Landlords' Protective League, a man of much dignity, suave deportment and faultless attire, who desired to be heard in opposition. Mr. Morrill of the Trade Club, another eminently respectable, dignified and well-dressed citizen, likewise desired to be heard in opposition. The representatives of a number of mercantile, financial and insurance organizations severally desired to be heard, presuming that their public spirit, respectability, wealth and well-known reputation for strict probity would have great weight with the committee, whose report, already prepared by Gentry, was in the hands of the Chairman, to whom it had been handed by Pop.

The faces of these eminently respectable, upright and fearless leading citizens were familiar scenes about the State House. Year in and year out they came before committees to oppose this job and that, only to be given leave to withdraw, and then to return to their respective clubs and trade associations, where they would receive resolutions of thanks for their unselfish and patriotic efforts, which in no instance (strange to say?) were ever crowned with success. Their opposition to any measure was always hailed with delight by the various committees, since it assured them that a fight (even though ineffectual) was to be made, and that meant "stuff" for the boys.

Of course the hearing proceeded as a matter of form. Mr. Denning made one of his characteristic saponaceous arguments, which was referred to in the papers of the next day as a "concise, cogent and patriotic appeal to the members of the committee in behalf of a great public improvement." He told his hearers that the glory of a people, since the days of Greece and Rome, was in its public works; that the consolidation of the various water companies would prove a blessing to the consumers of water, would do away with the expense of the several separate organizations, save unnecessary salaries, and so reduce expenses that the new company would be enabled to furnish water at a materially reduced rate. He pointed out that no restrictions should be placed on the amount of the capital stock, because it could not be definitely ascertained for how much the stock in the several companies could be purchased, neither could it be learned for how much a controlling interest in such companies could be obtained; that must be left to whatsoever trade could be effected between the parties. Curiously enough he did not advert to the fact that promoters care not what dividends can be earned for the widows, guardians and trustees whose stock subscriptions they seek, their only interest being in the marking up of the capital in the sub-companies which they mean to control and dispose of to the new corporation at exorbitant figures. Another case of "oppressing prudently."

Of course the several aforementioned "respectable, upright and well-attired citizens," who appeared in opposition, fulminated great truths that had been formulated by the founders of the government, quoted from the Federalist, referred to the Virginia and Kentucky resolutions and endeavored to impress upon the members of the committee (now engaged in answering the enquiries of their various constituents as to the chances of obtaining this or that office) the sacred duty that was vested in them to protect society and the dear old Commonwealth from the harpies who were seeking its life blood by this gigantic stock-watering job, — and the hearing was closed.

The committee then went into executive session, and the bill, which Mr. Gentry had drafted, with the amendment suggested by Mr. Birdinan, was agreed to be reported in the House the next day. In the meantime nothing

was to be said about the action of the committee until after the evening and next morning
newspapers had received their bite for publishing in full the "able, eloquent and patriotic"
address of the Hon. Mr. Denning. Of course
Mr. Wilkes was given leave to announce the
result of the committee's deliberations to his
principals, which he did without much delay.
Among the spectators at this important hearing
was Mr. Miles Mulvenna, who took careful
notes of all that had been said on both sides.
There were also present a large contingent of
the "third house," who eagerly watched the
various members of the opposition ranks,
hoping some one of them would require the
influence of such service as they might render.
Mr. Wilkes, of course, was everywhere, and as
he left the committee room with a beaming
countenance, flushed with the pleasure that
certain victory alone can give, he was hailed
with expressions of enthusiastic endearment by
a number of Senators and House members,
who, desirous of "catching on," had awaited his
appearance with marked anticipation, trusting
to be signalled out for his favor, like harlots
expecting their summons.

"Say, Wilkes," said one of the House members to the worthy lobbyist, putting his arm
affectionately around the former's neck, "are
you on this water case"?

" That's a leading question, is n't it "? replied Wilkes. " I never answer such."

" But say, Wilkes, there are about six or eight fellows who sit in my division that will vote as I say if we look after them properly. Otherwise they 'll holler, and holler loud, too. I 'm giving you this tip for your own advantage."

" Well, I 'll see you later; I 'm in a hurry now," said Wilkes, trying to shake him off.

" All right," went on the persistent member, " am I to understand that I 'm on, and tell the boys so "?

" Tell.them nothing; I 'll see you later."

" There are six, seven, eight, yes, nine of us. Now, don't forget it."

" Forget nothing."

Wilkes was hardly clear of the intruder when Representative Number Two attacked him with, " I 'm glad you 're on that water case. I 'm glad they got some one who understands business. Say, the 'gang' want me to act for them, so we understand each other, do we"?

" Understand nothing."

" I suppose, as usual, a hundred apiece "?

" You lie low, Mike, and say nothing till I know where I am."

" But the boys are hungry, and told me if it was not settled to-day they would fight the bill and kill it when it comes into the House."

" Do you suppose I am going to give you

my word, when I 've no authority to do anything"?

"That's all well enough to talk, but when
those water fellows hired you they knew it
meant 'stuff' to the boys. Now, no bluff,
Wilkes, we 're dead onto you. It won't do this
year to hire part of the 'gravel train' and not
all. We 'll make a fuss, and then there 'll be
an investigation."

"You are a fool. I always take care of the
'train' when I can. I 'm in a hurry now, must
run."

"When can I see you"?

"Say, Wilkes, *I* want to see you a moment,"
said a third, who thought Mike was consuming
altogether too much valuable time. "Our
county is all solid for anything you want, only
we will not be 'goosed' as we were last year
on the gas matter. How much will you make
it a head"?

"I won't say a word now," trying to disen-
gage himself from the country member's grasp;
"heavens and earth, what do you take me for ?

"Why, you can't put through a bill like that
without its being 'greased.' You 're too old a
coon, Wilkes, not to know that. I 've got to
say something to my crowd. Now, what will
it be, a hundred each, eh"?

"Don't bother me now; later I 'll talk with
you; there, there, I must run."

"Wilkes," "Wilkes," "Wilkes," chimed in several belated members.

But Wilkes had disappeared and was hurrying down the State House steps, leaving the impecunious and hungry crowd looking disconsolate. They all wanted the promise of Wilkes. His promise was good. Wilkes' capital lay in the fact that he had never broken his word in any financial arrangement, even if he had to make it good out of his own pocket. Principals might default, Wilkes, never. There was the secret of his strength.

The Metropolitan Water Supply Company had won its first victory, and when the following day the bill was reported, the purity press (the publishers of which had received the whole of Mr. Denning's speech for insertion at advertising rates, while the reporters had been properly looked after by Mr. Wilkes) united in praise of Mr. Morgan's executive ability, and dwelt on the lasting benefit that would enure to the public from his unselfish course in offering to give the people cheaper and better water. The water in the stock was not referred to by these guardians of public opinion, except by the Millville *Democrat*, whose reporter, familiarly known as "Parson Donlan," had not been fortunate enough to be on intimate terms with Mr. Wilkes. The opposition of the Millville *Democrat* was always considered an omen of good fortune as regards the passage of any bill. "If the Millville *Democrat* is against the bill, I 'm for it" was the cry of the average legislator.

Having learned that the committee would surely report the bill, Mr. Gentry immediately bethought himself of the best means to awake opposition to its passage. "Now," he said to himself, "of course I have Mulvenna under my thumb, but I need some one of rather more intense respectability, on whom I can rely to further my plans. There is Frederick Mambrino, he is a Dartmouth man and I can talk with him. It 's his first year on the hill; he can make a name for himself by following my suggestions. He is young at the business and probably has made no direct connection with any one as yet. I might as well get in with him and do his business for him as any one else." Gentry knew that prudent and shrewd politicians never let themselves down to but one man, every one else is rebuffed; so in this way a reputation for purity and integrity may be easily acquired, with larger returns as the result. It is only the light-weights who will do business with everybody, excepting always from this classification, Mulvenna, who was a law unto himself. "I 'll ask Mambrino," Gentry mused, "to call at my house to-night on some Dartmouth matter. Then I shall get him to

agree to offer an order of investigation into the
methods employed by the water company in
promoting legislation. That's it. That's it.
There's no danger of my trick being dis-
covered. Pop will know nothing of it; Denning will know nothing about it; Wilkes is
a sphinx and never heard of my being in the
case. The investigation, of course, will end
in smoke. There will be a large fee for
stifling it, and Mambrino can be looked after
at the right time, notwithstanding his virtue."

"Here, boy, deliver this letter to Mr. Mambrino; his office is right round the corner on
Washington street."

When Mr. Mambrino (member of the Reform Club and leading director in the Citizens
Association for the Purification of Politics)
called at Mr. Gentry's imposing Back Bay residence, he was greeted by the host in what was
supposed to be a very hospitable manner, but
the tone of the voice took from the uttered
words all semblance of geniality. Try as hard
as he might to play the princely entertainer,
Gentry failed to impress any one with the feeling that he was really glad to welcome him as
a guest. Essentially cold, sordid and selfish,
nature had denied him gifts which might enable
him to hide his real self. Notwithstanding
his dinners, parties and drives, no one ever
thought of calling Gentry a good fellow; that

he was a remarkably learned and accurate lawyer, everybody admitted.

"Before we go into the library, Brother Mambrino, have a glass of wine. I rather pride myself on some wine I have here. This came from London Docks, and it was only after a great deal of persuasion, and by really the importunate requests of some friends of mine, that I was able to procure it, and then only at a pretty stiff price, I assure you. It's of the famous vintage of 1822. This is Madeira," emptying the liquid slowly into a finely cut wine glass. "See, it flows like oil. Then the bouquet of it, why, it is superior to the oldest French brandy. Just try a glass. Sip it and enjoy the aroma. Did you ever taste anything like that"?

"It's delicious."

"Delicious, I guess it is. It's all that and more. Now take a couple of these Lord Portchester Elina cigars. They are a fit match for the wine. Never, Mambrino, my boy, smoke a cheap cigar after tasting such nectar as that. Appropriateness in all things. Here's a light. Let's go into the library."

For a while they dwelt on old Dartmouth reminiscences and formulated plans for the further spread of her well-known influence; then laughed at the feebleness of Harvard's favorite sons, and winked at each other as they

mentioned the various offices of State, from
the chief-justiceship down to the veriest process server, all held by Dartmouth men.

"Mambrino," finally spoke Gentry, "there's
a great chance for you to make yourself a
name, reflect honor upon our Alma Mater, add
to your law business, and stamp you as one of
the very leading men in this city. I can't do
such a thing, I should get myself disliked.
But you, with your youth and earnest desire to
be known by the public, have an opportunity
rarely offered to any one to distinguish yourself."

Mambrino was all attention.

"I understand the committee on Mercantile
Affairs will report that water bill. It's a dangerous, bad bill. It's the worst form of stock
watering imaginable. In my judgment it never
could have gone through that committee without the most barefaced bribery, and it can
never pass the House without the most shameful distribution of boodle. It is needless to
have much evidence on that point, though I do
know of one man who will make an affidavit
to certain circumstances, and they are enough
to start on. When that bill is under consideration by the House and looks as if it were
going to pass, you rise in your place and make
a most indignant protest against the passage of
the bill. I will furnish you with a brief.

Charge openly the wholesale bribery of members; allege that the committee was bought,
and back up your statement by saying you
have the facts to prove it. Put it as strongly
as you can. In truth, the more you insult your
fellow-members the greater will become your
reputation for courage and probity. You must
put it strong. No 'ifs,' 'ands,' 'buts,' and 'perhaps,' but the rankest sort of positive assertion;
gibbet them, one and all. An investigation
will of course be ordered, then you can show
your legal talent by working up your evidence.
You can get your witnesses from the weak-
kneed individuals who, thinking you know
more than you really do, will, in order to turn
suspicion from themselves, reveal to you the
offers that have been made them and the
rumors that are afloat. The average legislator
is a coward; so the more you frighten them,
the darker the insinuations you can advance,
the greater the evidence that will be freely
offered you."

Mambrino was delighted. He was to lead
the charge against corrupt practices. He had
been selected for that duty by one of the older
members of the bar, a man of the highest legal
reputation and unquestioned social position,—
the future was his own. Still, all this meant
work, and work of the hardest kind. So he
restrained his ardor and hesitatingly suggested

to Mr. Gentry that although he was exceedingly flattered by his signalling him out as the one to make this attack, yet he recognized he was undertaking a big load, and that it would take the whole time of more than one man. But Gentry quickly put that doubt to rest, by assuring Mambrino that he, Gentry, was president of the Good Citizens Club, that the club realized that the only way to purify politics was by some such great effort of reform like this; that no man could afford to give his whole time to such a work, and while the club would not for a moment suggest any financial consideration for a man's vote, yet for all that, it was perfectly proper that for all his extra labor and trouble Mr. Mambrino should be duly recompensed, and he, Gentry, would answer for that. The recompense should be commensurate with Mambrino's well-known talents and character, and would be a fit return for the splendid effort he certainly would make. "Good-night," said Gentry, as he ushered his guest out of the door, "you know the ground and how to till it best. Only do not under any circumstances mention my name as at all connected with this plan." He closed the door and smiled. "It came very easy," he mused, "how old Morgan would swear if he could have overheard this conversation. All this is business, strict business. I have a

pretty big establishment to run, to say nothing
of the drafts Madge Styles makes on my pocket-
book.   I must live, and the expenses of living
require a good many double fees.   I shall need
all the money that can be squeezed out of old
Morgan's syndicate.   No one will ever connect
me with this business.   I have been pretty
circumspect.   Pop's theory is correct, 'oppress
prudently,' 'oppress prudently.'   This is not
only the 'science of government,' as he calls it,
it is the science of nutrition."   And Mr. Gentry
sought his couch, and slept soundly the sleep
of the righteous and just man that he was.

CHAPTER IV.

A NIGHT OFF.

It was about two weeks after the occurrence of the events narrated in the last chapter that Pop, walking homeward from court with Judge Patchen, was startled by a most peculiar street cry. Who! o-o-o-o ah-ah-ah!

The noise was made by clapping the hand repeatedly over the mouth and rapidly removing it. The voice was feminine. The cry was borrowed from some variety performer, and, as it broke upon the still, chill air, was enough to arrest the attention of the most absorbed passer by. Pop looked up. He knew but one woman who would have signalled him that way; and disengaging himself from the Judge, whom he assured he would certainly rejoin in a minute, Pop darted into a large open doorway, where stood—in all her beauty of face and form, that had fascinated so many men — Madge Eugenie Styles.

"O! Pop, I am right glad to see you. I suppose you'll think I have nerve when I tell you what I've done; but I couldn't help it. It's awful, I suppose you'll think "?

"Madge, you dear girl, I never knew you to do anything that was n't all right."

"My! ain't you a flatterer! I'll tell you what it was. You've heard me speak of Mrs. Hanks, that poor widow who is a friend of Ma's? Well, she is in lots of trouble. Her only son, Jimmie, has been arrested. I don't know what for, and I don't believe she does. But it's some sort of a scrape, and the case is to come up in the police court to-morrow morning. He is down in the jail now, and she is almost wild. She's a really good woman, Pop, and Jimmie is her sole support. I told her — now you'll forgive me, Pop, won't you? — that I'd get you to defend him to-morrow, and that it should not cost her anything. I am sorry; but, really, I could not help it, she was in such a state. Why, it made me cry. You won't be mad, but you will do it, won't you"?

"Ah! Madge, who could refuse you anything."

"But you are n't very angry, old chappie, are you"? her brilliant black eyes swimming with tears, and her cheeks crimson, as she thought of poor Mrs. Hanks, and reflected on what she had done.

"I will look after him, Madge. Don't worry. But what's the news"?

"Another mash, Pop."

" That is n't anything new; nothing surprising about that."

" O, stop now, ain't you funny "?

" Who is the latest victim of those eyes "

" Say, did you ever hear of this swell from the South who stops at Parker's — his name, let me see, let me see, it 's Cherrie, Colonel Cherrie "?

" I know whom you mean."

" Just think of the cheek of the man. Why, I 've never seen him and yet he 's written me two or three letters, which of course I never answered. And then the impertinent cad went and laid in with the policeman on the street, and as I was going to Mrs. Hanks' — say, Pop, she *is* a good woman — the cop stopped me on the way and said he thought it would be a good thing for me to meet his friend Colonel Cherrie, a rich Southerner, who was a mighty liberal man, and that I would not regret it."

" What did you say to that request "?

" I told him that at present, such were the many calls on my time, I was not extending my list of acquaintances south of Mason and Dixon's line. So he laughed and went his way, saying simply, 'you are a star, Miss Styles.'"

" The patrolman told the truth. You *are* a star, Madge."

" But just think of this Colonel Cherrie; why, I am told that 's all he does — travelling round

and flirting with some one else's girl. I know
of two or three men who mean to ask him to
'put up his dukes.' He'll get a sound thrash-
ing some day. Did you ever hear of him"?

"I know of him. He's a Southern speculator who comes here to unload his schemes on
an innocent and unsuspecting public. Sometimes it's marble, other times it's land, then
sandstone and, perhaps, Southern mortgages."

"Gracious, I don't want to know any more
men. Pop, don't you think I've known enough
for one life? Say, wouldn't Gentry be mad if
he knew about it? I don't know how it is, but
I always tell you everything, Pop, don't I? I
can't help it, anyhow. You don't like Gentry,
do you? any more than anybody else does, do
you"?

"I like him only for one thing — because he
likes you. That's the only creditable thing I
know about him, and I don't blame him for
his attentions. If you could see Mrs. Gentry,
dressed *décolleté,* with her wrinkled and pow-
dered face, flat chest and scrawny arms, you
would not wonder at Gentry's admiration for
your ample charms."

"Hush – sh! *Ain't* you sweet"!

Gentry had married his wife for her father's
money, of whose estate he was now trustee.
When a tolerably ugly woman, who is simply
rich, returns the pretended affections of one

who is not so, she is simply a fool and deserves to be married for her money. The husband has deceived her, to be sure, in his protestations of regard which he did not sincerely entertain,—another instance of the wisdom of "oppressing prudently." It should excite no sympathy for her. A woman should have some perceptions.

"Say, Pop, I *have* something to tell you that *is* rich. When Gentry was up at the house the other night, it was last night, he was quite communicative for such a reticent gentleman; and having come direct from some festive gander party, where he had absorbed more than his prudent nature should have allowed him to take, and was in fine fettle and very communicative, his tongue did clatter like a mill wheel. He told all he knew regarding everybody. He is a shrewd schemer; say, he is smart. He's counsel for the water company, and at the same time he is putting up a job on it, his own client, through that conceited darling, Mambrino."

Pop affected not to be interested.

"O! You listen, Pop. I'm going to tell Gentry that he must hire you, and, old man, you touch him for a right smart fee."

"No, no, never mention it to him. I would rather not be in the case." Pop was doing considerable thinking.

"Well, if you don't want to make a dollar, why, don't blame me."

"You 've forgotten one thing, Madge. You invited me once to come up and dine with you and your chum Lizzie. I am in a mood for it to-night; and, honest Indian, Madge, you must not give it away for the world, I am going to bring with me my friend, Judge Patchen."

"All right. Come up. I 'll send a wire to Lizzie. She 'll come, sure. Say, Pop, she 's a dead game sport. I 'll tell you what 's better still: you order the food and I 'll bring the table fixings, and we 'll have the dinner in your 'growlery.' That will be a new experience for us, and for the 'growlery' as well. Will you agree to it"?

"Anything you say, goes."

"All right. At your 'growlery,' 6.30 sharp. I 'll be there."

"I will have the janitor keep the lift running till then."

"You won't forget about Jimmie Hanks"? And she raised her veil, leaned toward Pop, quickly kissed him, and, waving a 'bye-bye,' was off.

Pop rejoined the Judge. He was silent for a second as he thought on Gentry's double dealing, which had become second nature to that worthy. "Well," he said to himself, "let 's be charitable to Gentry; perhaps he can't help it. His fate may control him, and he is not to blame.   As I know his tricks, I may be able to circumvent him without exciting his suspicions or arousing his hostility."   So, putting his arm through that of the Judge, he trotted along gaily, a sort of hop, skip and a jump, chatting brightly all the while.   The Judge strode along, sombre, pompous, and wise.   And when, looking out of his wearied eyes at Pop, he expressed the wish that there might be at times some relief from the required dignity of the ermine, told how he would like to be gay and freehearted once more, and really get out of life a little of the sunshine, Pop improved the occasion by telling him he *should;* intimated to him how foolish this assumed gravity of judges was, and that it was a flimsy judge who was unable to arrive at a correct decision except through impressive gravity.

"Nature is joyous, the rivers ripple as they run to meet the ocean, the fields laugh in their fertility.   The necessity of gravity in a justice is a mistaken notion.   There is nothing serious or strained about nature."   Pop slapped on the back the dignified jurist (whom no one ever dared to address jocosely), and exclaimed: "You shall know it again.   You shall be a boy again just for to-night.   You are in my toils. I will give you just a taste, a sip, a wavering suspicion of Bohemia."

"Nay, nay; I have my opinion to write in

that intricate litigation of Witherspoon *vs.*
White, and must read it at the opening of the
court to-morrow."

"You will write all the better opinion after
a little relaxation. Let the mind drift in
fresher channels and the easier it recuperates.
To-night you are mine, absolutely mine." And
then he told the Judge that the beautiful girl
from whom he had just parted, with a friend
of hers, equally jolly, though not quite so much
of a stunner, dined in his quarters that night,
and the Judge must, no excuses accepted, be of
the party. Although the Judge promised to be
there, Pop was somewhat fearful of the keeping
of that promise, and as a hostage for its per-
formance grabbed the green bag from the
jurist's hand, promising to return it when the
owner showed himself at 6.30 in Pop's growlery.

It was 6.30. The Turkey-red draperies
were drawn and lent a warm, cheerful air to the
room, while the sputtering kettle, hanging from
the iron crane in the wide fireplace, made
music all the while. The logs burned brightly
and threw grotesque and fantastic lights and
shadows on the grim sheep-covered law books
on the wall. Pop was engaged unloading a
messenger boy, who had brought from a near-
by restaurant a huge basket filled with eatables
of all kinds, raw and cooked, from oysters to
game, from salads to ices — not to mention

several suspicious-looking bottles whose necks peeped out from beneath the blue-checked covering as if to see what kind of a place this was to which they had been brought. There was another basket resting on the table, containing table cloths, napkins, plates, platters, knives, forks, spoons, pepper and salt sprinklers, and what not, all carefully packed by Madge Eugenie Styles, who was to follow the basket in a few minutes, as the errand boy who brought it informed Pop.

A sound of footsteps in the hallway, a " Well, I suppose this is the Judge. I am Madge Styles, and this is my dear friend, Lizzie Ralston; we 'll introduce ourselves," and the door of the outer office opened and Judge Patchen, attended by two as attractive-looking beauties as one might see in a lifetime, entered. Madge, with her splendid carriage, superb figure, and sparkling, soulful eyes. Lizzie Ralston, plump, laughing blue eyes and masses of light hair, done up in a most bewitching twist, occupied the foreground, while the portly, grave Judge Patchen formed the background of a picture which Pop long remembered, and which now caused him to drop his work and clap his hands with delight, shouting lustily, " Bravo! Bravo!! Bravo!!! It 's 6.30. The eatables, guests and host are all on time to a dot. You girls, Madge, must set the table and get everything to rights, while the Judge and myself look on and criticise. Roll up your sleeves, Madge, like a true domestic, and pitch in. I want the Judge to see that peerless arm."

"Well, I guess not. When Lizzie and I have everything arranged for the feast we 'll call you, not till then. You and the Judge can wait in the other room and smoke."

So the Judge and Pop smoked and discussed matters in general, and law in particular, in the outer room, while Madge and Lizzie busied themselves in the "growlery" setting as inviting a looking table, even to decorating it with flowers, as a Lucullus would wish to behold; and, before long, everything was in apple-pie order and the invitation was extended to the worthy limbs of the law to enter and partake of the feast. Madge seated herself at the head of the table in Pop's stiff-backed wooden chair. Law dictionaries and encyclopædias were placed in the seats of the easy chairs so as to allow . the occupants to sit up close to the table, and then the tinkling of glasses, the clatter of plates, the music of knives and forks began. Madge was in her element, and even the Judge began soon to relax and enter into the spirit of the occasion.

"It takes a long time, though," thought Pop, "to wash out those fixed and judicial wrinkles which have been gathering for these twenty

years; but, if anybody can do it, Madge can."
And he hurried on the fun.   Between the
courses, Madge recited and sang, while Lizzie
plunked on her guitar, which she had brought
with her.   And the fun began to grow very
entertaining to the legal guest, so that after
a while he was encouraged to tell one story,
and then another, and at last even was prevailed upon to sing a song, which he did in
capital style and won the hearty applause of
the party, who insisted on an *encore*. "That's
it, that's it," cried Madge, "make the Judge
keep doing it till he gets it right."   And they
all laughed and joined in a chorus.   More
pounding on the table with the knife handles,
more drinking of bumpers to the Judge's
health, more songs, more guitar strains, and so
the game went on, each one growing merrier
all the while.   And then they called on Pop
for a recitation, and he gave them Hartley
Coleridge's " Amor Delixit," and as he repeated
these lines : —

> " She sat and wept, and with her untressed hair
>   Still wiped the feet she was so blest to touch ;
> And he wiped off the soiling of despair
>   From her sweet soul, because she loved so much,"

all were silent, and Madge wiped away a
coming tear with the corner of a napkin, and
for a moment everything was hushed. " Let's
not have anything quite so sombre," suggested

Lizzie, and then she went to work on her guitar with "Way down upon the Suanee River,"
and "Dixie," and "Maryland, my Maryland."
And the Judge gave them "Marching through
Georgia," and all joined in the chorus; and fun,
laughter, and general good fellowship prevailed.
The judicial wrinkles were fast disappearing
and the Judge was quickly becoming a boy
again. The kettle kept sputtering, the logs of
hickory burned brightly and threw their weird
shadows on the wall. Madge retailed the last
bits of gossip from the clubs, the Judge sang
and sang, Lizzie kept her guitar hustling, Pop
was radiant with smiles and bubbled over with
good stories. The end came all too quickly.
It was approaching the late hours, and the two
witches intimating that the hour had come
when they must be going, the Judge became
loud in his protestations of enjoyment at the
evening's success and insisted that Madge and
Lizzie must allow him to make them some
present for the entertainment they had afforded
him. But this was frowned down by their
suggesting that the pleasure was all on their
side, and then the Judge, looking fixedly into
Madge's eyes, said, "I am going to give you one
of the choicest possessions I own, as a tribute
to those eyes" ("Oh! how like they are to
hers," he thought), and he produced a gold
pocket-piece, on one side of which was the

head of Napoleon the Great, on the other the superscription had been removed, as only the word "Mispah" appeared. "This from me," he said. "The coin is a rare one and the circumstances under which it was given me are sacred. You remind me of the giver; poor girl, she died long ago, I suppose."

Madge turned the gold piece over in her hand, her long lashes wet with tears.

"Why, what's the matter with the Judge"?

Whether it was the heat, or the wine, or the sumptuous repast, or the memory of the past that affected the Judge was not apparent, but he had slipped from his seat, and was now half under the table, breathing heavily.

"He's all right," said Pop, "let us lift him on the lounge and put him away for the night. He'll be all right by morning. 'If he sleep he shall do well,' you know." So they gently raised him, laid him on the lounge, covered him with a thick shawl, tucked Pop's ulster round about him, and there he slept in the flickering fire-light,

> "Like a warrior taking his rest,
> With his martial cloak around him."

"I like the Judge; he's a good boy," and Madge stooped over the slumbering jurist and kissed him. "Now, you're a witness, Pop; his mouth is open, that means a pair of gloves — Chanuts — for me."

"You don't get ahead of me that way"; and Lizzie Ralston, kissing the open mouth, suggested that six-button gloves were the kind she always wore. "That will break a fiver," thought Pop.

"Good-night, Pop; and you will remember to send home the napery, and so forth, and, above all, don't forget Jimmie Hanks to-morrow morning."

"It's awful good of you, old chappie. Say, Pop,"—kissing him,—"we could n't get along without you. Ta! ta"!

And the pair put on their wraps and were gone.

Pop stood with his back to the fire, gazing at his sleeping guest. Then he thought of the "opinion" the Judge was to deliver in the morning, and laughed. "There will be more 'law's delays,' and I the cause of it. How his nibs will look at me when he wakes and thinks of that 'opinion.' This is too good to be true. —Here I have been interfering with the majesty of the law." And he laughed again. "By Jove, I have it. I 'll write that opinion myself. Egad, that is an idea," he mused. "If I can't write a better opinion than most of them, I 'd sell out. When old Patchen wakes up he shall have his decision all made for him, and typewritten to boot." So he swept away the debris from the table, brought pens, paper and ink, emptied the Judge's green bag, and set himself to work deciphering the memoranda the Judge had made in the now famous case of Witherspoon *vs.* White.

"Now, what fools these judges are," thought Pop, as he pored over the documents. "Here is the first draft, probably of an opinion on a perfectly plain case, and it occupies twelve pages of manuscript, filled with all sorts of 'ifs,' 'perhaps,' and 'buts,' references to this judge's decision and that court's qualification, citing an authority here and explaining away an objection there. Oh, what nonsense! Three pages ought to suffice. It's nearly all rubbish. I'll put this in shape, and it shall not be more than three pages in length, either." Scratch, scratch went the pen, down came this book from the wall and back went that one; now this passage was stricken out, and then something else inserted. Scratch, scratch went the pen, the big logs smouldered in the fireplace, the Judge snored on the lounge, and the opinion was being boiled down in great shape. It was almost done, and Pop, as he read it over critically and admiringly, looked at the Judge, laughed, and said to himself: "Now, once more I'll go through it and apply the 'labor of the file,' and away he went, striking out prepositions, articles and adjectives, until he brought the long decision within three pages of legal cap, when he rushed into the other office, unlocked the typewriter's desk and put the decision in Witherspoon *vs.* White in proper form for the court and laid it on a chair by the side of the sleeping jurist. The dawn was showing itself in great lines along the horizon, and Pop gazed down the harbor at the lights which were one by one being put out. Still the Judge slept. Pop munched some of the bread and fruit left from the feast, and contented himself with the thought that he might as well make his breakfast there as anywhere, then, as any time. " I wonder what he meant by giving Madge that pocket-piece! The old fellow was quite overcome, too; some little romance, may be. They all have them. Sometime it will come out, I suppose, and then the world will know the skeleton in *his* closet. Ah, me! it's all in a litetime," and he stood looking out the window at the sea and the ships and the lighthouses, lost in a day dream.

If any one for a moment suspected that Madge and Lizzie went directly home, it was a mistake. The last-mentioned Miss was, as Madge styled her, " a dead game sport," and the idea of going to bed without further libations was farthest from her thoughts. So, of course, Ober's was the destination; and finding a number of congenial spirits engaged in making things look different from what they are, they joined the party, and more revelry was the result.

When Madge arrived at her flat in the small hours, she was in what would be called a truly glorious condition and still was hardly able to give an accurate account to her mother of just where she had been. To the anxious en- quiries of the old lady, she only made answer: "Shjudge" — "Pop" — "Liz Ralston" — "Ober's" — and sank into a chair and slept. Her hand grasped tightly the pocket-piece that had been given her earlier in the evening.

"What's that? What's that"? said Mrs. Darby, as she caught sight of the glistening gold, and took it from the sleeping beauty's hand. A hurried look at the coin, a glance at Madge.

"My God, girl, where did you get it? An- swer! Wake up! I never thought I should see it." Frantically she shook the sleeping one for an answer. Madge only breathed heavily.

Another long, wild, frantic gaze at the coin; then, turning it over and looking at the other side with "Mizpah," she cried: "It is the same," and fainted.

The Judge still snored on Pop's lounge, un- conscious that the past and present were so near together. There is no such thing as time.

"Wa, wa, why, where am I"? said Judge

Patchen, as he tried to rouse himself, and stared about him in a wild sort of fashion.

"Just where you have been for the last twelve hours — no difference," said Pop, who was intently awaiting developments.

"Oh, Pop! Pop"! looking at him reproachfully; "my opinion, my opinion."

"Can't be worth much to judge from your Honor's present appearance."

" But what shall I do? I adjourned the court to this morning, simply for the purpose of rendering my decision, and now, now what excuse can I make"?

"None, except to read your opinion."

" But I have not written it, where is it"?

" Right on the chair, my dear sir, all ready for delivery; what more do you want"?

He grasped the typewritten document, scanned it rapidly by the light of the fading fire of the smouldering logs, and eyed Pop with astonishment.

" Have you done this"?

" Is n't it all right"?

" Well, I can't help laughing, but it 's better than I could have done myself."

" Unquestionably. I never cry down my own wares. But why is n't it all right"?

And the Judge read and reread it again and again, and said it was all right.

" I 'll admit," said the lawyer, "that there is not in that opinion the profuse allusions to

Hennecious and the Laws of Oleron, to say
nothing of Chitty and Coke and the statutes of
Elizabeth, to which you fellows on the bench
are wont to garnish your opinions. But I have
been honest. I have had the grit to rule
something, and then have refrained from quali-
fying it all away. It is plain. He who runs
may read. It can't be cited hereafter as an
authority on both sides of the question. And
I have n't tried to steady myself by elaborate
references to the labors of the Commissioners
to revise the statutes. But it's law, it's common sense, and it will stand."

"Pop, I don't quite comprehend what has
happened and how it has all come about. But
you are a jewel, and they won't know how it is
I was able to write so good a decision. It is a
difficult case. It has troubled me a good deal,
but you have made it plain as day."

And Pop made a low bow and put his hand
to his heart, with mock gravity, enjoying the
situation immensely all the while.

That opinion in Witherspoon *vs.* White, so
exact and yet so simple, so concise and yet so
full, so compact and strong, brushing away all
legal technicalities, and with unerring analysis
marching at once to the real question in issue
and deciding it with one blow, long remained
an evidence of Judge Patchen's legal ability,
and was the inciting cause, some months afterwards, of his elevation to the Supreme bench.

"But to change the subject, who is this Madge Styles? Did I give her that pocket-piece? Well, I can't help it now. Those eyes, those eyes."

"Well, Madge is a charming widow."

"A widow"?

"Oh, yes, her husband was a worthless fellow, who turned out a gambler and drunkard and went to the dogs shortly after his marriage."

"But the family, who are they? Has she a mother? What's *her* name"? he asked eagerly.

"I've forgotten her mother's name, strange to say, though I have a case for her. But the father was a bright, witty, reckless journalist, who years ago was shot, and her mother struggled along till Madge's marriage, and after *her* husband's death, well, well, I suppose it's no secret, Madge has supported the family since, and I don't say it was always with the profits of virtue; but she educated her brother, he's at Oxford now, really living on the money she sends him, although he is in ignorance of it, thinking it comes from some annuity to which his mother is entitled. Madge keeps him at that distance, so he may not understand the real situation of affairs."

"Then they are Americans," interrupted the Judge, somewhat relieved.

"I suppose so. But, Judge, she's a splendid

woman just the same, for all her faults, if you choose to call them such; honest, warm hearted, full of fun, and I need not say anything of her beauty and style, need I "?

"Beautiful eyes, what eyes she has got," and then he mused, looking into the dying embers and calling up in memory the long-vanished past.

"Yes, Madge is a trump. I've known her a number of years. She is always the same, always. To be sure she is not one of the "Four Hundred," but then I fancy that when the Almighty strikes her trial balance at the divine exchequer there will be a tidy sum to her credit."

"Well, well, I suppose I must go to breakfast as soon as I can make myself presentable," trying to shake himself together and assume a respectable and dignified appearance, for which he was always noted. "I dined with you, now come and breakfast with me. I can't promise you so good a time, for I *have* enjoyed myself amazingly, and it's made a new man of me. It was a great experience."

But Pop could not accept the invitation. Jimmie Hanks was at the jail and he must see him at once, before he was brought up to court. So the Judge picked up his papers and went his way, while Pop scurried down to the jail, through the crowd that at that hour in the morning swarms through Court and Cambridge streets to its daily avocation.

The few minutes previous to the opening of the courts is always interesting. The court officers are hurrying to don their blue coats and brass buttons, the criminal lawyers are surrounded by the bootblacks who will give them the only polish they will have that day, the big caravans from the jail are drawing up to the sombre building and unloading their human freight, forgetful attorneys are giving their parting instructions to the officers who are to serve their process, the clerks and students are approaching with the green bags and yellow-covered literature of their masters, who will themselves follow later at a more deliberate gait; red tape and parchment are universal; every one has something of the utmost importance on his mind.

On this particular morning a number of "eminent counsel," as they are called, were grouped at the front door of the Court House watching their brethren at the bar as they passed by, and criticising them with that all-knowing judgment which ever distinguishes the successful attorney. Their eyes fell on Pop, who was approaching them at a rapid gait, and the fire of criticism began.

"Curious chap, that Ormond," said one, quizzically.

"Should say he was," remarked Augustus
Harrison, Esq., the well-known authority on
equity proceeding, "something wrong about
him. When a man gets to be forty years of
age and is n't worth anything to speak of, there's
a screw loose somewhere."

"He tries a case pretty well, though," said
Lloyd Hopewell (an insurance attorney who
never hesitated to pump what law he could
from Pop), rather apologetically.

"Try a case well, yes, a cheap one, accident
or poor debtor," answered another, "but he
accomplishes nothing. No railroad, bank or
insurance company would think of employing
him."

"And yet he's possessed of a pretty good
mind, gentlemen," broke in one of the clerks
of court who had overheard the conversation.

"I judge a man by results. That's the only
way to properly estimate a good lawyer. He
may be able to make a stump speech, but a
lawyer, bah"! This was Mr. Harrison's ulti-
matum as he broke away from the group and
looked contemptuously at Pop, who was now
passing between the greasy, swinging doors of
the police court room, intent upon doing what
the Prophet and Master had done before him
— to save the widow's son. Spirits of Elijah
and of Christ! In that other day, when the
seals shall be broken and the judgment that is

writ shall be rendered, shall it not be more tolerable for this man than for those, his critics, to whom on this earth God Almighty in his mysterious wisdom may have awarded the un-earned increment?

CHAPTER V.

Mr. Wilkes had completed all arrangements for a successful termination to the first skirmish the adherents of the Metropolitan Water Supply Co. must encounter. He had selected two members from each division in the House to be present at the first reading of the calendar and keep accurate account of those who cried "pass." He had also assigned two or three of his underlings to similar duty in the galleries. For those legislators who were too timid to indicate their pretended hostility to a bill by direct attack in the manner of speech-making and debate, preferred to signify their desire to be seen by "passing" the bill when its title was read. After the adjournment of the day, the various members and agents reported to him the list of names they had secured, when he compared them carefully, tabulated them as to ability, influence and cost, and then made a memorandum, after consulting with upright, patriotic Mr. Denning as to which ones he should communicate with before the opening of the next day's session. This course was pursued every day, each day the number of "passes" growing beautifully less under Mr. Wilkes' careful attention. At first as many as thirty different members shouted "pass," but by the end of a week it had dwindled down to two or three scattering and feeble cries. Mr. Wilkes, therefore, announced to Mr. Denning that the time had arrived for taking the bill out of the orders for the day and making a special assignment to a day certain when all the forces should be in readiness for the battle.

A distinguished concourse gathered at the State House on the day assigned. Large stockholders in the new enterprise, speculators in stock, owners of patent devices, authorities on water supply, delegates from the various citizen and good government associations, wended their way to the Capitol in such numbers that lookers on wondered "what was up" that day. Justin Bulrush Morgan was the cynosure of all eyes. As he passed through the halls and corridors on his way to the Representatives' Chamber, the whole lobby, that had arranged itself like a procession waiting to be reviewed, bowed very low (the more forward of them thrusting out their hands for recognition, that they might excite envy in the minds of their less fortunate brethren), and expected Mr. Morgan would at once hire them, as their influence was potential. But Mr. Morgan did not appear

to have ever seen the gentlemen, and his recognition did not seem to be particularly fervid.   In
fact, he had studiously avoided the members of
the third house, leaving all such business to
Mr. Wilkes, in whom he had entire confidence
after the flattering recommendation Pop had
given that eminent worthy.   Mr. Denning,
knowing the crowd he should have to encounter, in which were many old political associates,
entered by a back door, and before anybody
could get at him, seated himself in the rear
part of one of the galleries, where he could
escape observation and yet be a spectator of
all that took place.   Mr. Wilkes, like the good
general he was, kept himself in the background,
having deployed his agents in various parts of
the chamber and through the corridors, who
were to report to him in the temporary headquarters he had fitted up in one of the many
lodging houses opposite the State House.
The least observed, the least enquired about
of all the throng, was Frederic Mambrino, Esq.,
though he was destined to be the central figure
in the contest that was approaching.   The
"lobby" always avoided Mambrino.   He was
known as a civil-service reformer, a tariff tink-
erer, a correspondent of the *Nation*, a member of the bar committee on expulsion, and an
occasional contributor to the Millville *Democrat*
on such subjects as " Municipal Purity," " Polit-

ical Morals," Right and Wrong in Government," and all such subjects, so attractive to
the callow mind.

The debate followed the lines laid down in
Mr. Denning's "cogent, concise and patriotic"
address to the committee. The different
members of the committee were very eager to
have an opportunity to display their abilities
before Mr. Morgan, knowing that in a few
months they would cease to be members, and
then the Metropolitan Water Supply Company
might retain them as attorneys or agents.
When the debate dragged a little, a raw-boned
Yankee in one of the divisions near the Speaker's desk, was seen to rise slowly and look
toward the Speaker as if about to lay some
weighty point of order before him for consideration. A smile passed over the assembly, for
all knew what was coming. This gentleman
was universally known as the mover of "the
previous question." His legislative duties
never went beyond this, and he never allowed
any one to anticipate him in this regard. The
House was ready for the question, especially
the members of the "gravel train," who, knowing
that the only way to recover their fee was to
be recorded on the yea and nay vote, had been
in their seats for two hours,—something that
was remarkable in those gentlemen and creditable to them in the highest degree.

Without a moment's warning, before the mover of the previous question was recognized by the Speaker, a shrill voice shrieked "Mr. Speaker," and Mambrino rushed into the area in front of the Speaker's desk.

"I am surprised, Sir; I am mortified beyond the power of speech to describe; nay, I am profoundly shocked, when I consider that such a wicked, dangerous measure like this, fraught with disaster to the dear old Commonwealth, whose best interests I have so deeply at heart, should be allowed to become a law without some protest. If I stand alone, it makes no difference, I will at least discharge the duty I owe to my conscience, my country and my God." ("God" was mentioned last.)

What *was* coming! The reporters in the gallery grasped their pencils and set themselves busily at work; the members ceased their reading and chatting; the lobby rushed by the doorkeepers and peered through the oval glasses in the swinging doors leading into the chamber, delighted at what seemed to them a turn in affairs that might bring them trade; the members of the Mercantile Committee hurried together for consultation; Mr. Morgan looked astounded; the smile vanished for a moment from Denning's face and lighted on that of Mr. Gentry, who sat in the reporter's gallery, crouched behind one of those hard-

worked scribes. One did n't have long to wait
for the *dénouement.* Mambrino passed from
one clause of the bill to the other, then attacked
the counsel for the petitioners, hurled his shafts
of indignation and scorn at the complete power
that shameful Mr. Wilkes had wielded over the
committee, and then, with a sweep of his hand
and glaring from one part of the chamber to
the other, he cried aloud: " Bad as all this is,
it's nothing in comparison with the wholesale
purchase of members that this villain of a
Wilkes has engineered on the floor of this
House." (*Sensation in all parts of the chamber.*) At this time Mr. Wilkes was quietly
seated in his headquarters, smoking his after-
dinner cigar, and wondering why those fellows
across the way would persist in so much
" talkee, talkee."

" I speak none too strongly. I hold in my
hand," waving a sheet of legal cap which
appeared to be covered with writing, " the
proof of all I say, the affidavit of a well-known
man, to the fact of the base bribes that have
been offered, and in many instances, I blush to
say, accepted "!

One by one members of the " gravel train "
passed out and quietly disappeared from the
building. The committee looked troubled at
the thinning lines, fearing they might not be
able to stand any test vote. And Mambrino
continued,—

" I had hoped in the midst of all rumors that have been floating for the past month through this State House (as a matter of fact there had not been a solitary rumor afloat, not even a breath, as it were, of suspicion, except the dark glances and unfounded insinuations one William McGonigle, a third-rate lobbyist, had scattered about when he ascertained his services were not needed by Mr. Morgan), some member of the committee would, for the preservation of its own dignity, have moved for an investigation. They sit silent under these charges. I therefore move such action on the part of this House, and as testimony of my disinterested efforts in this matter, decline to serve on the committee appointed for such purpose."

The committee on Mercantile Affairs uttered never a word. They sat in their seats as if mastered by some narcotic poison. The House turned toward Mulvenna. He rose slowly, his face was sombre as a churchyard, his voice hollow as the grave; one hand was in his trousers pocket, grasping tightly the roll of bills little Daniel Morgan (the president's son) handed him just before the opening of the session, the other was extended toward the Speaker, and in slow and solemn utterance he expressed the hope that the motion would prevail, and that, too, without a division on the vote. Then he roused himself, and lashed those who would be so false to their oaths as to sell their vote,— the most sacred possession a man can have given him by his fellows. He would not use such strong language as his young friend who had just sat down had employed, although he was not sure but what it was justified by the event. He always feared the end of the Republic would come through the undue influence of corporations, and, for that reason, had always fought them, and tried to educate the people, so as to destroy the pernicious influence of these soulless bodies. Then he waxed warm on the necessity of obedience to the great moral sense in all human affairs, showed how the moral law, though often warped and twisted, was never broken. And he sought to throw light on the ruins of past nations, all brought about by the prevalence of corruption in ancient times.

" Look at Phœnicia, with its great commercial depots of Tyre and Sidon. Once she was at the very height of power and ruled the world eight hundred years before our Christian era. But it was a nation of shopkeepers, and its morals, religion, official power, as well as its goods, were for sale to the highest bidder, and so its life went out. Alexander the Great conquered it, its great metropolis was burned to the ground, and this harlot of nations left nothing to history and posterity except the fact that the commercial spirit had been carefully

educated in its domains. Phœnicia lacked
that supreme ethical element in civilization
which alone suffices to ensure permanence in
the life of a nation. May no such ending ever
be the lot of this country or of this Commonwealth! And the way to guard against such
disaster is to stamp out every attempt at corruption, however and wherever found." And
he seconded the motion for a committee of
investigation. Of course it was carried without a vote against it. Young Mr. Morgan,
white as a sheet, stood in the men's galleries
like one turned to stone, as he listened to
Mulvenna's words. Could he believe his
senses? This man who had hounded his
father day after day, who had been paid twice
over and then wanted $500 more, because the
pressure on him from Millville to vote against
the bill was so great, and *he*, young Danny
Morgan, had himself handed the $500 to him
only at the opening of the session. What
did it mean? It was a dream, certainly. No,
there was his father down stairs surrounded by
the members of the Committee on Mercantile
Affairs, expressing their sympathy, assuring
him that it would come out all right. There,
too, was Denning, without his eternal smile.
What did it all mean? He would see this man
Mulvenna at once, and demand back his
money. He evidently did n't understand Mul-

venna. Mr. Mulvenna was leaving the chamber as he approached him, and hardly recovered from the stupor he had been thrown in by the sudden turn of affairs, young Mr. Morgan began in rather a dazed fashion by enquiring why Mulvenna had not kept his bargain, as he agreed to do if he was paid that $500? For a moment the air was what they call "blue." Mulvenna was towering in his rage; he seemed ten feet tall, and glaring at poor, inoffensive Morgan, he turned on him like a tiger.

"You scoundrel, what do you mean by insulting me in that fashion? Who are you, anyhow? If I did not think you were some deluded crank sent here for a joke, you would be behind the bars in a mighty few minutes. I pity you. Some one has been playing with you. Here, Mr. Sergeant-at-Arms, here is some crank that will bear watching." And he marched off to the coat room.

The lobby was delighted. "Now they will see our power. It will be a good lesson to this man Wilkes. He'll find he can't get along without us," was the characteristic remark made by several of the third house. Parson Donlan of the Millville *Democrat* was equally delighted. His eyes of horn twinkled and his heart of steel throbbed as he contemplated the rare opportunity that was now offered him to crucify Wilkes and to ridicule Denning. Donlan always mistook malevolence for virtue, and here was a chance to show to the world his lofty ideals of moral worth and to preach a newspaper sermon on corruption and wrong-doing, in which he would have the aid of his admirable acquaintance, Mr. Mambrino, whom he would laud to the skies.

The friends of the bill which had been so mercilessly shattered were somewhat crest-fallen. They gathered round Mr. Morgan and tried to offer suggestions as to the best course to pursue. It was the opinion of all that a protracted council of war was necessary, and that the Committee on Mercantile Affairs, with leading members of the House and Senate, should meet Mr. Denning, Pop and Wilkes for the purposes of consultation. Mr. Morgan, in his liberal, off-hand way, thought the best place to meet was at his house, where all would be welcome to dinner, and as Morgan's dinners were known to be very elaborate and his wines especially choice, there were no dissenting voices to this proposition. Mr. Morgan then smiled on his admirers, assumed an indifferent air as regards the day's result, and, bidding all a very polite "Adieu," jauntily passed out of the chamber.

Morgan was a fair type of the poor prairie boy who rapidly accumulates a fortune in the West and then comes eastward to display his wealth and offer instruction in the art of money-making. From cowboy he had become herds-man, from herdsman he had risen to the dignity of cattle dispatcher on a single-tracked railroad, then superintendent of an abattoir, and lastly, the head of a pork-packing firm, from which he had retired, having amassed several millions. Having been informed of the advantages in an educational way to be derived by a prolonged stay in the Hub, he had removed his family to Boston, sent his son to the Boston Latin School and then put him through Harvard, while his daughters had attended the most fashionable private schools in the city. His large wealth had brought to him opportunities to serve as director in several national banks and trust companies, while his name was always mentioned when any one spoke of the railroad magnates of the country. He accepted all the offices tendered him. He knew it brought him in communication with many bright and fashionable men, association with whom must destroy many of his own boorish ways and manners. In fact, he was readily welcomed at the most exclusive clubs, and his social success was only another instance of the truth of the aphorism that the possession of approved bank and railroad stock makes remarkably good blood, at any rate in the New England metropolis of culture.

Mr. Morgan's dinner that night was not a dress-coat affair.   In fact, the only ones who were in full evening dress were Pop and Wilkes. Mr. Denning always refused to go to any entertainment where swallow-tails were a necessity. He liked to be known as belonging to the "plain people," did not hesitate to tell others so.   If it were known that he had ever worn a dress suit, it would render his well-known influence at cattle fairs of very little account. Mr. Morgan himself was resplendent in a gorgeous wide-flowing scarf of many colors which covered two thirds of a very wide shirt bosom, which in turn was enclosed in a fancy velvet vest, across which was suspended a massive gold chain, and from which hung all manner of charms and masonic emblems, the whole supported by a pair of distressingly light trousers that rested on gaiters of the same material, covering shiny patent-leather shoes.

"Solomon in all his glory was not arrayed like this," said Pop, as he nudged Mr. Wilkes, who was somewhat "flabbergasted," as he afterwards expressed it, by the gorgeous apparition that seemed to pervade the whole room.

"Shall not we, need some one to present us to so august an object"? whispered Wilkes.

"The pork packer on his throne, is he not? Well, it's hardly fair in us, Wilkes, to criticise, when we are going to drink his wine and are

already under his retainer; but, really, when a
man with such complexion and such colored
whiskers does not know that there is only one
kind of a necktie that nature will allow him to
wear, to wit, plain black, he deserves harsh
treatment." Before Pop could proceed further to elucidate his ideas on dress, Mr. Morgan,
recognizing his two faithful lieutenants, reached
out both hands and welcomed them cordially.

" The two men we are waiting for; now we
shall get wisdom, and lots of it"!

And everybody wanted to shake hands with
Wilkes, and, on the sly, whisper in his ear the
question, whether this defeat of to-day would
make any difference in the contract they had
made with him. To which several interroga-
tions Mr. Wilkes winked, and whispered back,
" Lie low and say nothing." And the mind of
the enquirer was thereby relieved, and Mr.
Morgan, with his extensive tawny whiskers,
or rather bristles, sandy complexion, pimply
forehead and expressionless eyes, was again the
centre of attraction. His upper lip was shaven,
and gave him a sort of purified-through-trial
smile, such as Knight Templars affect when
they lead their forces through the streets on
St. John's day and cast a pitying glance at
the admiring crowds upon the sidewalk.

And yet, as Pop afterwards admitted, Morgan
was a good fellow, a real good fellow, but his

style killed him. His idea of correct costume was to dress like a gambler or sidewalk masher. Yet he was neither. A good neighbor, a good business man, a warm-hearted, kind friend, he suspected nothing wrong in others, and was as open as the day himself. Still, he *would* dress in his own fashion, and, as it injured no one but himself, the world laughed and became used to it. But the dinner to which the company were shortly bidden was a wondrous affair, more wonderful than Mr. Morgan's wonderful costume, more varied, more costly, and as dazzlingly captivating as his watch chain, and more so. It was a melody, a symphony in food and wine, to which the markets of Savannah and Baltimore, Washington, New York and Boston had all contributed their rarest offerings. So far as politics was concerned, no conclusion was arrived at, no course laid down, no plan agreed to. In this respect it was the same as all political dinners—nothing accomplished. The committee, of course, had no very definite ideas on any subject at any time, and after the third course was removed those straggling attempts at ideas seemed to be removed also. Mr. Wilkes, though often requested to state his views, claimed not to be very familiar with exactly what did take place that afternoon, and wanted time to think it over, while Pop preferred to get at all the facts after he had talked with Mr. Morgan later. Still, it *was* a rousing dinner, and the members of the committee, with several friends that they had invited on their own responsibility (a custom more honored in the observance than in the breach with members of the Legislature), all voted Mr. Morgan the most princely of entertainers, and vowed him their eternal support on any measure he might wish. This last promise annoyed Mr. Wilkes, and on rebuking one of the gentlemen later, he pointed out the great mistake he had made. "Do n't promise anything in the future, otherwise they won't feel it necessary to 'come down.' Get your pay separately on all matters. Never connect entertainments with more than one specific vote." Wilkes wanted the legislators to get all they could. He took large fees himself, but he wanted his friends in the State House to do well too, and so feel like coming another year to the General Court. It was a correct business proposition: always use your customers well, and Wilkes' customers, both buyers and sellers, could be numbered by the hundreds.

When all the company save Pop and Wilkes had departed, Morgan hurried his two remaining guests into his private library, locked the door, and then turning to them said, almost despairingly, "What must be done? I can trust you two fellows, or at least I can trust

Pop here and he swears by you, Wilkes, I can assure you." As a matter of fact, Pop and Wilkes were not very intimate, and neither knew much about the other, but Mr. Wilkes possessed certain qualities that always aroused Mr. Ormond's admiration, while in turn Pop was possessed of certain faculties that ever evoked Mr. Wilkes' enthusiasm. Pop was never flurried, and under fire was as cool as a cucumber; besides, his royal good fellowship had an infinite attraction for Wilkes, who was a trifle deficient in that respect. Pop liked Wilkes because Wilkes always looked at things as they are, always studied facts, and never surrounded situations with unmeaning sentiments. Mr. Morgan sat in his library armchair, Mr. Wilkes occupied the sofa near by and placed one hand on Morgan's left knee, while Pop, who was mounted on a stool side of the latter, had his hand on Morgan's right leg. Their three heads were close together, and Mr. Wilkes began to lay down his views with his usual vim.

" Now, let us talk business and do it quickly. You've a mean fight ahead of you and I must have *carte blanche*. The committee will be a joint committee of fifteen, and not a House committee of seven. For I understand this Mambrino attacked the committee, which is joint. Every man in that Legislature will want to be on that committee, since it means spoils: they will squeeze you hard, and from the beginning will 'signal for stuff.' The gravel train will want their pay doubled, and those Senators I have secured will feel the price agreed on is too small. What is wanted is money, money, and lots of it. You had better let me have ten thousand to-morrow morning as a starter. The result will be all right. No fear about that."

And when Mr. Morgan agreed to all that was necessary, but expressed a desire to know just what "signalling for stuff" and "gravel train" really meant, Wilkes informed him that Pop, who was a better talker than himself, could explain all that. As for himself, he never was acquainted with the merits of any bill, did not understand them, and only did what he was told was wanted, defeat or passage. An important engagement would now make it necessary for Mr. Wilkes to leave, and Pop would answer any questions, and would, no doubt, explain everything more satisfactorily than he, Wilkes, could himself, and excusing himself, he left Mr. Morgan and Pop alone in the former's library.

Cigars were lighted, and Pop informed Mr. Morgan that there were many men in the Legislature who desired to be "seen," as the phrase is, and as they might not be on intimate terms with the parties in charge of any

bill, it became necessary to communicate with
them by signals which would convey an assur-
ance to the various agents that their offers
would be entertained. Sometimes such legislators contented themselves by shouting " pass,"
at other times they moved an adjournment, an
indefinite postponement of the bill, or told the
agent to his .face that they were " agin him."
Mr. Morgan took it all in, making no reply, but
at the same time wondering if this was what
Lincoln meant by " the goverment of the people, and for the people, and by the people."

As to the meaning of the phrase " gravel
train," Pop said there was a double meaning
attached to that. The " gravel train," pure and
simple, referred to a couple of dozen members
of the House who were on no important committees and had no special influence, but who
by combining together, could make quite a
formidable array of votes. When there was a
large private bill, as in this case, other members of the Legislature, who were not on the
committee reporting the bill, joined the gravel
train, and for their votes received the same
price. And when Mr. Morgan informed him
of all his troubles, and how this member and
that Senator had been to see him and made
all sorts of suggestions, and recommended this
lobbyist and that as the proper one for him to
consider, Pop smiled and told him he was

going through the usual experience. That he would have to pay out sluices of money without hope of return.

"Pay, pay, even if it realizes no results, pay. Buy them and rebuy them, and keep buying them. Waste your money if it becomes necessary. You will have two hundred men on your pay roll before you get through; not one in ten will do you any good, still do it, pay, waste the money if need be. Make no fuss about it.

"Be like a ship on the ocean. A good ship may leave a wake behind her, but she makes no waves at the prow. That's my advice, *make no waves*. Do as Wilkes says, let him run it. Follow his advice in every particular."

"But what a daisy this man Mulvenna is," said Mr. Morgan. "Why, sir, he is a dead-cold 'boodler,' I believe you call it. He insisted on calling on *me*. I never sought the fellow. *He* came to *me*, at *my* office, and the first question he asked was, 'Now, there is no need of preliminaries. How much do I get'? I have run Western towns and I have bought Western legislators, but nothing like this did I ever see. He's a highwayman, and he followed up this question, when he saw me hesitate, with 'You know what I can do with any bill that comes before that House'? And when I replied that I did, and tried to taffy him a bit on his ability, he simply looked scornfully at me and hissed out, 'Fudge, fudge,' snapping his fingers in my face, same as a robber might cock a revolver. And then he drew back and stared at me for a moment and attacked me thus: 'Don't you understand? I do not come down to Boston every day for fun, and my health is pretty good, too. You'll give those committee men all the way from five hundred to a thousand. I'll take the latter figure, but I want to do my trading here, at the home office. Don't refer me to any attorneys. I don't know how good your word is; you're a stranger at the State House; suppose you give me that sum now'? And, Mr. Ormond, I am ashamed to say it, I did, I gave him the money," and Pop laughed.

"O! yes, Miles is a keen one."

"That isn't the worst of it, that isn't the worst of it; he kept coming to my office every other day, and finally said the money he had received was altogether too small, and d — n my eyes, if I was not fool enough to give up another thousand." Pop laughed again.

"I know him of old, he's a *rara avis*."

"The worst is to come. He was at my office again this morning, representing that his Millville constituency were howling because he had not gone before the committee and prevented the reporting of the bill. I did the best to hedge off, but he *is* a clinger, and the

only way I could get the d——d nuisance
out of my office was to promise to send
him $500 more before the opening of the
session, and I sent my son up with it. The
rest you know. Why, I have shot my man on
those prairies, fought Indians, river thieves
and road agents, but they are not in it with
this man." Pop threw himself on the lounge
and roared, and roared till the tears flowed from
his eyes in streams.

"It's no laughing matter, I assure you.
This is the best specimen of a Massachusetts
legislator, if I read the Boston papers correctly.
They all speak of him affectionately and
point with praise to his great services to the
State. I do not care for the money, but I do
know that no other State but Massachusetts
would allow such things. You fellows in the
East cry out if once a year a railroad train is
held up by Western bandits; but this man is
allowed to prey on the community and blackmail them out of thousands every week, and
your civil-service reform editors do nothing
but sing his praises. It's an outrage, sir, I
tell you. Out West they would form a vigi-
lance committee and hang this fellow to a sour
apple-tree quick, and don't you forget it."

And Pop kept on roaring, and the roaring threatened to become contagious, for Mr.
Morgan had used up a great deal of vital force

by the explosive manner in which he had related Mr. Mulvenna's visits and expressed his
own indignation, and there was opportunity for
a reaction.   But he quietly chuckled, and intimated that it was no use to cry over spilt
milk, though this was a very queer sort of a
Christian Commonwealth.   And when Pop
tried to moralize with him, he refused to hear
him, at any rate at that time.   When this investigation was over and there was no damage
done, he would be glad of a social call from
Mr. Ormond, whom he had grown to like
more and more, each time he saw him, for he
did believe he was honest, and he was not saying the same of everybody in Massachusetts.

CHAPTER VI.

COLLARING THE BOODLE.

It is needless to remark that Mr. Gentry felt pleased over the prospect of an investigation, sent Mambrino a check for a comfortable amount, and personally congratulated him in behalf of the citizens generally for his courage in defying the powerful combination he had to meet.

And Mr. Mambrino walked the streets more erect than ever; he was never very humble in his carriage. At the clubs, that evening, he was treated with the greatest deference; and, in fact, so pleasing had this wholesale commendation become, that he desired its frequent repetition, and even condescended to strut through Young's the next Saturday, when the lobbyists and newspaper men might see him and murmur to each other, "There goes Mambrino"! Not less pleasing was the plethoric retainer the Good Government Club, as he supposed, had forwarded him through Mr. Gentry.

The investigation, of course, proceeded as usual. As nearly every member of the Legislature wanted to be appointed on the com-

mittee, the presiding officers of both branches
were in a state of great complexity. Mr.
Gentry while urging, as his duty to his client
demanded, the names of several who would be
faithful to the interests of the water company,
took particular pains that Mr. Mambrino should
see to it that there were men put on the committee whom he could control. After much
pulling and hauling, the presiding officers were
in such a quandary that, taking two or three
of the names suggested by Mr. Mambrino, they
practically allowed the persistent Mr. Wilkes
to name the rest. It was thereupon announced
in the press (the Millville *Democrat* excepted)
that the President of the Senate and Speaker
of the House had made the best use of the
material at hand and had appointed a very
strong committee, one, in fact, that would be
free from improper influences of any kind.

When Wilkes was enquired of as regards the
complexion of the committee, he professed the
greatest ignorance of the matter and intimated
that he scarcely knew the names of those who
had been placed thereon.

On the first Saturday succeeding the order
for an investigation, Mr. Bill McGonigle, to
whom reference has been made in another
chapter, dressed himself as sprucely as his
limited wardrobe would allow, spent his last
dime on a very fastidious bootblack, and took

his place near the radiator in the main corridor of Young's Hotel.

On this particular afternoon Mr. McGonigle was smiling and suave, more so than his usual custom. He retailed to everybody, who was willing to speak to him, all sorts of scandals, political or otherwise, about every prominent man that might be enquired of. Whether what he said was true or false made no difference. He rattled it off so rapidly that after hearing him talk for five minutes one would be completely exhausted, if he had not already became utterly nauseated, with his wholesale attempt to cover everybody with mud and slime. But it was particularly this characteristic of McGonigle's that appealed most strongly to Parson Donlan's choice nature. The "parson" always made it a rule to send to his estimable sheet a political letter for its Sunday issue. The more malicious and libellous the better, the more it pleased the publishers of the Millville *Democrat;* and the reservoir which always supplied him with an unceasing flow of scandals, innuendoes and falsities of every description was the Saturday afternoon communication which Mr. Bill McGonigle imparted to him, with such unction, such regard to detail and such fulness of authority. If the steady country people, who were in the habit of reading this lovable correspondent's letter,

imagined that it was simply a compilation of
" Bill " McGonigle's diatribes, they would have
revolted.   Not knowing this, they swallowed
the information as gospel truth, not believing
that the good publishers of so good a newspaper as the Millville *Democrat* would publish
anything other than the truth.

But now " Bill " McGonigle meant to figure
more prominently than ever.   Mr. Wilkes had
not employed him at all that year, in fact no
one seemed to want his services, and this had
wounded his pride severely.   That one who
had been such a "good every-day-working-Re-
publican," as he himself expressed it, should
now be thrown overboard, was rank.   Why, it
was to him that the great Nicholas Nathaniel
Nutbourne, the boss of Boston, owed his political training.   " Bill " did n't propose to stand
it.   So, as he poured his swiftly-running torrent
of abuse into " Parson " Donlan's ears, he in-
terspersed it with mysterious references to an
interview of which he knew, because he overheard it, that took place in a certain office,
when one of the committee, who was tickled
by Wilkes' generosity, admitted the reception
by himself of five hundred dollars.   " Just
think," went on McGonigle, " of this snoozer
to whom his legislative salary seems a fortune,
getting five hundred dollars at one clip,— five,
crisp one-hundred-dollar bills "!

"Terrible, terrible"! and Parson Donlan shrugged his shoulders and shuddered.

"And then openly bragging about it, too."

"Most corrupt state of affairs. Go on, tell me more," urged the reporter.

"Tell you more? If I wanted to, that is, if it were proper for me to give away my brother politicians, I could tell you things about this Metropolitan Water Supply Company lobby that would fairly sicken you. But I would n't. It is n't the thing to do. I never try to hurt any one," and he bowed and engaged in conversation with some one else.

The poison had fallen where it would do the most good. No other newspaper reporter would believe one word that McGonigle ever said. His lying propensities were so strong and so well known that whatever proceeded from him was at once discredited. Not so with Parson Donlan. He always reported faithfully anything McGonigle gave him, and added to it all manner of suggestions and innuendoes. This McGonigle knew, and his latest bit of information regarding the five-hundred-dollar bribe (wholly made out of whole cloth) would be found in the weekly letter to the Millville *Democrat* the next day. Then McGonigle knew that such a story would rouse the usually calm Wilkes, and that he should have the whole water lobby after him, to get him at the cheapest price to keep his mouth shut. The lie he told had a certain amount of reasonableness about it to be believed by many. The sum mentioned, five hundred dollars, was a very probable amount; and, if it should happen to be the exact amount, then Wilkes would be terribly frightened and surmise that he, McGonigle, knew it all.

And it all happened as McGonigle supposed. The lie was repeated in the columns of the Millville *Democrat.* McGonigle's name was given as that of the man who could substantiate the story, seeing that he had overheard the admission of the recreant committee man. There was consternation in the camp of the Water Supply Company. Telegrams went in every direction that Sunday. Mr. Wilkes was nimble. Denning shook his head in sorrow. Mr. Morgan stormed, and forgot for once Pop's advice about making "no waves." Mambrino was elated. With Gentry there was inward peace and satisfaction. But McGonigle — McGonigle, the "good every-day sort of a working Republican," as he always styled himself, McGonigle saw a fortune awaiting him at the hand of Mr. Justin Bulrush Morgan. And so easily made! No work about it. No toil. One great big lie in reference to a conversation he never overheard, and which, in fact, never existed at all. Twenty-five hundred dollars to shut up and clear out before the committee could summon him! He must insist on his price. If he asked less than such a sum, a doubt might arise about the truth of the story. And it all came about by reason of the malicious-minded Parson Donlan, who, in the exercise of superb purity, had spread it to the world. What luck!

It is unnecessary to observe that McGonigle had sized up the situation with remarkable perspicacity. The result, of course, was as he had foretold, only, after some higgling as to price, he came down to two thousand dollars, and on being paid the same, made due preparations for a "prolonged drunk" (it could be called by no other name, so bestial and filthy was it), which took place in Chicago, the length of which adumbration being about two calendar months.

What with Mulvenna and McGonigle, Mr. Morgan was fast exhausting the pleasure of having his leg pulled in the most approved fashion. What was coming next? There was that investigating committee. What would they insist on? What would be the demands of their uncles, their cousins and their aunts? He did not have to wait long in order to find out. That committee "got down to business" with surprising alacrity. Their first stroke was to hint to Mr. Wilkes that before any

hearings were had, a trip to New York, especially at this season, about the time of the
Arion ball, would be appreciated. Mr. Morgan, on being made known of this request,
groaned inwardly and begged leave to consult
with Mr. Ormond, and let the committee
learn of his pleasure later.

"We'll make it our pleasure, you bet," said
one of the dignified members of the committee
on receiving Mr. Morgan's reply through
Mr. Wilkes. Morgan had grown to have confidence in Pop's honesty and frankness and so
hurried up to his office with anxiety pictured
on every feature, to learn what a trip to New
York had to do with an investigation of the
methods of the Metropolitan Water Supply
Company. Pop assured him that it was not an
unusual thing in a committee, even if all the
members were rich men. In fact, rich men
more often demanded such attention than did
their less favored fellows, for nothing so attracts
a man who has himself made his pile as to
get something for nothing, say a pass to the
theatre, or a trip ticket to Washington. He
then explained that trips to New York were
orginally started by timid capitalists who felt
they could make their contracts with greater
safety in another jurisdiction. After a while
it was looked upon as a preliminary, to put the
committee in a frame of mind to be pleasantly
approached.

" If the committee ask for a trip, you will be
obliged to give it to them, or you will be har-
assed to death," was Pop's answer to Mr. Morgan's enquiry as to how to act. And so due
arrangements were entered into for conveying
the committee of investigation, numbering
fifteen souls, or, to speak more accurately, fifteen bodies, to the city of New York, there to
pass the space of two days in such a whirl of
pleasure and earthly delights as can only be
furnished by that enlightened metropolis. In
fact, Mr. Morgan himself began to look forward
with keen anticipation to the good frolic he
should have with the committee. He was a
sociable fellow, and made up his mind to make
all his guests have a comfortable time of it, if
food, drink, theatres and other *fin de siècle*
entertainments could accomplish such a result.

They were all to go in a special Pullman
buffet car, which had been stocked with the
choicest of viands and most delicate of wines,
not to particularize the most solacing brand of
cigars. Mr. Morgan was at the station betimes,
dressed in his usually offensive style, with one
of his own special neck handkerchief creations
that would have won the friendship of the
bravest of Indian chiefs. Mr. Wilkes was on
hand, too, busying himself with laudatory intro-
ductions of the various members of the committee to the princely host, who was constantly informed that this or that member was " one of

our kind." The appearance of the chairman of
the committee, the President of a small country
bank (accompanied by his two sons, estimable
young men, then studying at the neighboring
university), was the signal for applause and the
cause of a most elaborate introduction. He
grasped Mr. Morgan's hand, informed him that
he appreciated the invitation, thought it afforded a good opportunity for his two boys to
have a vacation, and so brought them along,
thinking it would be a pleasure for Mr. Morgan
to have them in the party. That worthy
thought differently, though he said nothing,
and simply ground his teeth and clinched his
hands at the exhibition of such extensive cheek.
But the chairman was not the only one to im-
pose on the good nature of the President of the _
Metropolitan Water Supply Co. Shortly appeared Mr. O'Toole of the North End and Mr.
McManus of the South Cove (members of the
committee), each having in tow a rather grew-
some looking friend, with prominent biceps
and *blasé* eyes, characteristic toughs of the several districts from which they hailed. Messrs.
O'Toole and McManus presented them as
" perfect gentlemen," who had attained marked
distinction in the prize ring and whom they
had invited to go along with them on the trip.
Mr. Morgan was getting a rather drastic dose.
He had arranged for accommodations for the

committee, a messenger, Wilkes, Pop and himself, and that just filled the special car he had
hired.   Yet here were four more for whom
provision must be made.   Besides that, the
clerk of the committee had invited a newspaper
reporter to accompany them, at Mr. Morgan's
expense, of course, and the only thing now to
be done was to ask that another Pullman be
attached to the special car, which caused some
delay in starting, and gave Mr. Morgan, who
was now thoroughly disgusted, the opportunity
to enquire of Pop if there were any more insults
to be heaped on him.   To which enquiry, amply
justified by the occasion, Pop laconically
answered :

"No waves.   Remember, no waves "!

As the various invited guests took their
places in the cars, Mr. Morgan drew Pop and
Wilkes aside and whispered, " I can't stand it,
boys, I cannot.   I am so provoked that I
could not treat them decently.   Here "(handing them each a large roll of bills), "you fellows
be paymasters; give them a good time.   Do
all that is proper, but I can't go"!   And he
darted out of the station, his face a study, dis-
gust and disappointment struggling for the
mastery.   He was hardly out of the building
when a man of a familiar face and voice, grip
in hand, and running at the top of his speed,
saluted him.   "Am I too late, old man ?   Has

the train gone"?   It was Mulvenna.   It was too much.   He could have felled him to the ground, but he remembered Pop's advice, — "No waves," — and without answering, turned in the other direction, and walked up a side street.   As he reached his office, a grinning, light-stepping individual came out, who extended his gloved hand to Mr. Morgan and informed him that his name was Senator Canter, and that he had put himself out to come way down from the State House to let him know of the desirability of having his affairs at the State House managed by Col. Nelson of Lawrence, a friend of Senator Canter, whose vote could, of course, be relied on, provided Col. Nelson was retained.   Mr. Morgan wondered if it would ever end.   Still there was Pop's advice, "No waves," and he restrained himself. In fact, he did more, — was polite, — was charmed to meet Senator Canter, — should like to meet Col. Nelson sometime.   Was quite busy then, and hoped Senator Canter would pardon him if he then excused himself.

The committee being in New York, Mr. Morgan supposed he should have a few days of quiet and rest from political cares.   In this he was wofully mistaken.   The absence of the committee simply afforded to those who were left behind opportunity they were quick in improving, to "get at" Morgan.   While the

committee were at home, no one else had a
chance to occupy his attention. But the committee gone, the chance was open to all. They
generally called in pairs, so one might corrob-
orate the statements of the other as to that
other's ability in managing such matters, and
his extraordinary "pull" with the House, and
especially with those members who composed
the committee. The lobby members also took
occasion in the absence of the committee, and
Mr. Wikes, to call on Mr. Morgan and
rehearse to his wearied ears the wonderful
manner in which various bills had been successfully pushed through, by reason of their
skilful tactics. Then came down from the
back country towns and hillside villages, sundry
antique-looking individuals, attracted by the
rumors of boodle that are always prevalent in
cases of investigation. These individuals
came to tell Mr. Morgan that they would try
to influence their respective representative,
whom they knew by meeting him at cattle
fairs, and would Mr. Morgan wish to hire
them? They were old-timers, knew all about
politics, kept up to the times by constant reading of the weekly *Journal* and the Old Farmers' Almanac, referred to this and that defunct
town heeler, whom Mr. Morgan must have
heard of and to whom they referred him.

So all these senators, representatives, lobbyists, heelers and politicians poured into the

offices of the Metropolitan Water Supply Company; they filled the air with smoke, spit on the carpet, left their tobacco cuds on the window sills and their cigar stubs on the mantelpiece. They all knew it all; all could do everything; Mr. Morgan had made a mistake in the men he had employed; he never could hope for success unless he employed *them*, and under the circumstances they would be as reasonable in their charges as one might expect. "The committee was bad enough, but would to God it would return and save me from these carrions"! thought Mr. Morgan, as all day long he was obliged to meet this throng and invent bluffs and schemes for putting them off,— no very easy task, as any one knows who has ever tried it.

At last the committee, somewhat the worse for the wear and tear of the trip, returned. Mr. Wilkes had learned the wishes of the majority of the committee as to recompense, notified Pop to meet him, compare notes and call on Mr. Morgan with reference to the final settlement with the committee. While the sums in all instances showed that they expected the largest generosity on Mr. Morgan's part, some, notably Mr. O'Toole and Mr. McManus, stipulated that Mr. Morgan should use his influence to get liquor licenses for the two friends who had accompanied the committee on its trip to New York. These two friends, prize fighters and "perfect gentlemen," had made enough money to retire from the practice of the manly art of self-defence, and not being attractive enough for the stage, determined to display their abilities behind the bar of a saloon,—as being the only trade that would sufficiently comport with the dignity of their position.

Wilkes and Pop compared notes and arranged everything in the form of a report to be presented to Mr. Morgan. As they walked down the hill, they noticed the sound of hurried footsteps, as if some one was trying to overtake them. Their pursuer was a tall, dignified personage, with snowy white moustache and imperial. He might easily have been mistaken for one of those German counts or barons who favor the Kurhaus at Continental watering places with their presence.

This elegant personage tapped Wilkes lightly on the shoulder and begged permission to speak with him a moment, and drew Wilkes aside. It was Senator Houghton. He winked at Wilkes, then expectorated, and with his dapper shoes spread the saliva on the pavement. In Yankee land, action like this is supposed to import great shrewdness on the part of the performer.

"Say," Senator Houghton remarked. "Is

there any stuff floating round? If so, just let me know." Another wink on the part of the honorable Senator, and he withdrew.

Wilkes, even Wilkes, looked petrified. At last he broke out "Whew! I am flabbergasted! What on earth do you suppose, Pop? That cuss was librarian at the Sunday school in his town, then became the Superintendent, and now is Chairman of the Prudential Committee of his church! and he has just signalled for stuff. My God, they all want it, don't they? Good Senator Houghton a boodler! Why, everybody looks up to him as perfection itself."

Pop showed no surprise. He simply intimated that in asking Mr. Morgan for funds, he, Wilkes, must include the necessary amount for the Christian Senator who had just informed him of his yearnings.

They were nearing Morgan's office, and Wilkes took occasion to remark to Pop that when they arrived there, he, Pop, should entertain Mr. Morgan with his stories and reminiscences and jokes till Morgan was in a good frame of mind, when Wilkes would produce the report and "touch" Morgan for the "requisite."

This plan was followed out to the letter, but when Wilkes produced his report and began the reading of it, Mr. Morgan's face grew sombre, and when the end was reached, and the gross sum total that was needed that day was named, he leaped from his chair, brought his fist down on the mahogany table and with an oath, shouted out:

"I thought the stockholders of the Metropolitan owned their stock, but now I see they don't. These legislators own it, and will allow us only to have just enough to keep it going."

"True," said Wilkes. "You have not been as long as most people in learning this. I'll take the check for that amount now, if you please."

Mr. Morgan laughed, and ordered one of the clerks to draw Mr. Wilkes a check for the amount asked for, and then began to deliver himself of his pent-up feelings on the "effete East" in general, and the Christian Commonwealth of Massachusetts in particular. Wilkes was constrained to listen, for the clerk was some time in making out the check. Pop told Mr. Morgan that his rhetoric was vigorous, but that waves would only impede the progress of the vessel.

"Well, I won't orate any more" (handing Wilkes the check), "but I will say just one word, and that is — Damn"!

CHAPTER VII.

HOW AN INVESTIGATION ENDS.

The investigation followed the usual course of procedure. Witness after witness was examined and cross-examined with the same results. They knew nothing. Had heard rumors, but nothing tangible had come to their ears. McGonigle, of course, was out of the way. He was enjoying the attractions of Chicago and studying the politics of the woolly West. Hearing after hearing took place, continuance after continuance was granted: the committee was known to be all right, but no report of its findings was forthcoming. All felt that the report must be unanimous in order to carry any weight. The moral effect of a unanimous and favorable report would go a great way toward passing the original bill: but the full committee could never be got together. There were always two or three absent members, and those absent members were invariably the gentlemen whom Gentry had, through Mambrino, succeeded in putting on the committee. It was already the middle of spring, and Morgan was daily growing more impatient for the end. Neither Gentry, Denning, or Wilkes could give him any reasonable explanation for the committee's delay. So Pop was consulted. When he told Mr. Morgan his view of the situation and that the only way to get the committee to report, though it was unpleasant for him to say it, was for Mr. Morgan to retain Gentry for that purpose, the President of the Metropolitan Water Supply Company opened his eyes, and burst into a derisive laugh.

"Why, man, he is already under my retainer"!

"I know it," replied the counsellor, "but that retainer was on the original bill of the water company. This is different. This is on the investigation. Like man, a retainer must be born again."

"Nonsense, sir, I tell you."

"And I say it is the fact," warmly replied Pop. "In my humble judgment this whole investigation was started by Gentry."

"I'll not believe it," said the President, "it's too monstrous for credence. That an attorney of high standing, already under his client's retainer, should so act as to demand a second retainer is without the bounds of reason."

"And I know it to be the truth," returned Pop, having in mind what Madge Stiles had remarked to him.

"This is too silly; I took you for a wiser man, Mr. Ormond. Good day," and he turned on his heel, resolving in his mind never to enter that office again, for he now was fully persuaded that Pop was as much of a trickster as any of them.

And still the investigation dragged its weary length along. Still the hearings were called and adjournments made. Everybody was tired of the whole business, but no report was forthcoming. Lobbyist after lobbyist tried his hand at the job. Nothing could be effected. The committee could not be got together, no matter how faithfully every member promised to be present. There was no report. It was already May. The grass waved in the State House yard. The trees on the common were shedding their blossoms, but there was no report from the committee. And yet the Legislature could not adjourn without action being taken on that matter. The President of the Senate, the Speaker of the House labored with the committee in vain. The whole committee could never be brought together. Where was the difficulty? In all this period of anxiety and solicitation, Gentry alone bore himself serenely. But the mystery was soon to be solved.

One warm, sunny afternoon in June, Mr. Morgan alighted from the elevator in the building where Pop's office was situated, and entered by the door whose threshold one month before he had vowed he would never cross again. Pop,

his hands crossed behind him, was looking out
the window at the steamers, the ships, the
yachts and small craft as they moved gaily
adown the blue waters of Boston Harbor.

"Pop, old man" began the President, slapp-
ing him on the back and stretching out his
gloved hand, "forgive me. I come to ask your
pardon. You were right. That bill will be
reported to-morrow. I have done what you
advised, and I made 'no waves' in doing it."

Pop turned his seer-like eyes upon him and
gazed enquiringly. "Come, I must tell you
the whole story. It's interesting, and bears out
the truth of what you imagined. We'll take
your sanctum." And in they went, Pop wondering what could have happened that should
have induced such a course on Morgan's part.

Pop dropped himself into one of the roomy
window seats which commanded a view of the
sea, while Mr. Morgan seated himself in one
of the arm-chairs, and proffered a veritable
Havana; and as he related his story, inter-
spersed it with throwing out large volumes of
smoke and delicate rings of nicotine vapor.

"You know," he began, "my son, Dan"?
Pop nodded, smoked his cigar and heard all
that was being said. "Well, some months ago
he became infatuated with a girl named Madge
Styles. She is quite a stunner, I assure you,
and, as such creatures go, somewhat respect-

able.   Nevertheless, it is not quite the company
I should select for him to keep.   Still, boys
will be boys, and I had rather have him sow
his wild oats now, than to do it ten years hence.
But he became so confoundedly stuck on the
woman, who was a few years his senior, that I
felt it was an acquaintance that it were best to
put an end to.   Hearing that the young woman
was a tolerably good sort of a being and possessed of brains as well as beauty, I made up
my mind to see her and have a frank talk, and,
if it was necessary, pay something to have
her give Danny up.   Of course this was without his knowledge.   So, day before yesterday,
I started for Madam's apartments.   Her rooms
are situated in a flat house, one flight up.   As
I was part way up the stairway leading to her
door, I heard the voice of a man that I recognized as familiar.   I halted and listened.   Being
a warm day, the door to her room was open,
and I caught every word.   Pop, the man was
Gentry.   I lingered long enough to hear him
say:

"'Well, my dear girl, if you only knew the fun
I'm having with old Morgan in this investigation.   If it keeps up a little longer, he'll tum-
ble to the game and I'll get enough out of him
to pay your expenses to Europe, if nothing
else.   The old cuss (that's me, think of it!)
will never dream of the fact that I've put up

this whole investigation. And I'm the only one who can stop it. But I must be paid for it, and I shall be.' I did not want to hear anything more. I departed. I was dumbfounded. Why, I supposed he was to be trusted. I had made my will and put him in as trustee, the scoundrel. Well, I thought it over that night, and slept on the whole matter. Then yesterday I called on him.

"'Mr. Gentry,' I said, 'I've called to retain you on this investigation.' 'Why,' said the innocent-looking schemer, 'why, Mr. Morgan, I am already under your retainer.' See how cunning the rascal was. 'O, no,' I replied, 'that was only on the water bill, this is a wholly different matter,' and I pulled out a big check and handed him, which I noticed he didn't refuse, but gave me a receipt for. And this morning I get a letter from him in which he says the committee will report this afternoon that the charges of Mr. Mambrino are not sustained and therefore no action is necessary.

"And there you have the whole story. O! I forgot. Mambrino, this civil-service reformer, has got to be attended to: I am to retain him as counsel for the new trust company I am forming. The place more properly belongs to you, Pop, but I've got to do it. According to Gentry, Mambrino must get *his* 'pay.'"

So the feet of the idol were made of clay.

Pop congratulated his visitor that the long agony was most over, assured him of the pleasure it had given him to be associated with a gentleman of Mr. Morgan's character, and hoped he might be able to serve him at some future time. And Mr. Morgan informed him that he should make it his business to throw what he could in Pop's way.

One week from that day the bill incorporating the Metropolitan Water Supply Company became a law, and everybody (except Donlan) forgot that there ever had been an investigation. Donlan alone cherished the memory of it and continually, during that summer, referred to it in his timely Sunday contribution to the Millville *Democrat*. By the way, let us be fair,— Donlan did not get anything out of it.

As Mr. Morgan passed out of Pop's office that afternoon in June, the postman entered and handed Pop a square envelope addressed in a bold, flowing feminine hand. He quickly tore it open. It read as follows:—

"MY DEAR OLD POP.:—

I am going abroad. I start next Saturday. Think of it! to be gone three months. Ain't I in luck for once? I want you to be sure and not forget Ma's case next week. I am not a witness, so I shall not be needed. I do hope you will win it.

But think of it, Pop. I am going abroad. I shall see all those lovely places you have told me about. I am going to Liverpool, where I shall see all those docks. Then I am going down to see that beautiful Devonshire County, where you said you once lived. I am going to see that street of steep stone steps in Clovelly that you sketched for me, and ride through the Hobby, and I will go and take that steamer ride on the River Dart from Dartmouth to Totness; and I then cross England to London, of which you have told me so much. O! I shall take it all in. I sha'n't forget to go to Greenwich, where poor Nell Gwynn founded that charitable institution for orphan boys, and I will eat some of the white-bait at Greenwich, and 'maids of honor' at Richmond in the Star and Garter, and a lark pudding in the Cheshire Cheese, near Fleet street. You see I have n't forgotten anything you've told me. I remember it all and I shall always remember you, dear Pop. Next to Ma, I shall think of your goodness to all of us. Now, I mean this, Pop. It is n't taffy. And then I go on the Continent, down the Rhine, through Switzerland, and I don't know where else. I am just excited, and I would not feel a bit provoked if you should think enough of your Madge Eugenie to send a little bunch of flowers for

her over to the Cunard steamer next Saturday.
Good-bye; don't lose Ma's case.

Affectionately,

MADGE EUGENIE STYLES.

P. S.— Gentry has had a settlement with
those water supply people. He says he made
them pay roundly. Say, he is smart. You
made a mistake you did n't let me work it for
you so as to get on to the case. Danny Morgan says his old man is sick of the 'leg pullers.' Excuse the use of the word 'leg,' but
that's what he said. Ta, ta! till I see you
again. *Au revoir*, is n't it?   M."

CHAPTER VIII.

A DAY ON.

A not wholly uninteresting character was Barney Garraghan, familiarly called the "undertaker." This name was given him from the extremely adept manner in which he managed the "grave yard" ward. Whenever any voter in that ward died, Mr. Garraghan jotted the name down on his list, and forthwith the name appeared on the voting list of some other ward, a sort of political as well as bodily resurrection. Garraghan's list at the time of this tale numbered some seven hundred names, the owners of which rested quietly in the cemetery. On election day Barney's gang, which comprised some two dozen choice spirits of the genus "bum," began the rounds of the voting booths, each voting on various names selected from the so-called "grave yard list." Only such precincts were selected as might contain a plethora of lodging houses, and no man voting in any precinct where he might be recognized. The pay the men received was small enough, for Barney kept for himself the larger part of the money handed him by Nicholas Nathaniel Nutbourne, the boss, insisting that the greatest

value should be attributed to the "list," of
which he was the sole custodian. The balance
of the year Mr. Garraghan devoted to the
duties of bill and rent collector, as well as the
service of petty process as constable, to say
nothing of the service he gave railroad and
railway corporations in the collecting and prep-
aration of evidence for accident causes. In
this latter line he was a genius. It was often
remarked that somehow or other his acquaintance was so extensive that no accident could
occur in any part of the city without there
being a witness to it who was on intimate
terms with Garraghan. His services were
therefore invaluable to the corporations.

On the night of the day on which Madge
Styles had sailed for Liverpool, Garraghan
might have been seen in one of the attractive
liquor palaces that fringe the streets leading to
a railroad station. The bar room was a bewil-
dering embroidery of mahogany and glass, of
electric lights and artificial flowers, of lager and
rum,— the fascinating dado with which civilization decorates the tapestries of time. He
was addressing two bleared-eyed looking be-
ings, who seemed to have some difficulty in
holding up the immense casks against which
they were leaning.

"Now, no more of this, boys," said Garraghan, looking at them in a threatening manner.

"Times is hard, Barney; don't blame us," said the more intelligent of the two.

"I know dat, and ain't I here for just dat purpose, to give you two a job? What are you talking about? Dere's plenty of biz if you only keep on deck and 'tend to it. Look at me; I am always round, picking up things for such as you to raise a dollar on. Pshaw! men, what cud yer do widout me? You'd starve, you would. Now, brace up, and have some style about yer. I want to talk biz."

The two stood a trifle straighter, stood closer to Barney, and endeavored to be all attention.

"On the third of last July you two might be going home from your work"—

At the word "work," Barney winked his eye, and the others answered with a horrid leer.

"And you noticed a woman dressed all in black get off of an open horse car, on de corner of Tremont and Berkeley streets. D'ye hear? Now, pay attention. And after she got off de car, both feet on de street, she caught her foot in the skirt of her dress and fell heavily on the pavement. Now it's a shame for railroad corporations to be bled."

Barney winked again. The two leered also, and nodded their heads.

"Nothing improbable in your seeing all dis, is there"?

The two shook their heads; the larger one seemed not to be so well pleased with the programme as Barney might have wished. So the undertaker pulled him by the shirt, and getting him in a corner between the cask and the side of the room, said: "Don't you be a fool. Dis is all right, I tell you. What do you care about this woman? She's a French Huguenot, or something like dat,—nothing you ought to care about. Dere's a fiver in it for each of you. Now, no nonsense. Go up to-morrow morning by daylight and see de place. You notice particularly how the streets run and get it all down fine. De case will be on for trial on Tuesday. Monday night you be here at nine o'clock to see me. Now keep sober. No drink. Here, I'll buy yer some corned beef for de old woman." So he dragged him and his companion to the neighboring market, and, purchasing two hunks of beef that looked as tough as the two individuals for whom they were purchased, gave each his parcel and sent them home with this caution: —

"Remember, now, you're positive about it. The woman was on de street, had left dè car, and was trown down by her own negligence. Do you hear"? An expressive wink. "You are to meet me in de 'Glass Slipper' (the name of the gin palace they had so recently vacated) on Monday at nine. Now, git home. Good-bye, boys." And he raised his hand patronizingly to them.

The two besotted creatures staggered off, ever and anon dropping their burden of beef, and then quarrelling as to the ownership of each particular piece. A looker-on would be witnessing the foundations of the fountain of Justice, and the law of evidence would have a new meaning for him.

Had Mrs. Darby, Madge's mother, seated by the side of her counsel in the court room, looked in the direction of the rear of the room, she would have seen Barney and his two keepers, for the profession which the two bar-room loafers followed was that of constable's keeper, and also in the political season played the role of adjutants in the undertaker's "grave-yard" regiment. All three were rather more decently attired than on the night above mentioned. Barney's Galway sluggers had received a fresh coat of paint, while his adjutants had only recently left the barber's chair.

Sitting in front of this admirable trio was a gentleman of eminent respectability, whose intellectual visage proclaimed him a member of a profession whose grade was considered vastly higher than the calling followed by Barney and his aids. Yet was he also destined to play the assassin as well as they in the cause about to be heard. He was the medical expert who, for his regular expert fee, was to declare that Mrs. Darby was shamming, and that her statements as to her injuries were grossly exaggerated. This he would do in such a manner, and with so persuasive a voice, that even his Honor on the bench would be profoundly impressed with the truth of his opinion, nothwithstanding the professed disbelief in experts which judicial arbiters are wont to entertain.

The attorneys for the defendant appeared as arid, uninteresting and vulture-like as most corporation advocates. They wore an air of extreme unconcern, and took their places at one of the tables behind a fortification of law books and green bags.

Pop, alert and self-poised, watched the jurors as they filed into their seats, and whispered to Mrs. Darby which ones would be apt to be favorable to her cause, and which were understood to be defendant's jurors. Barney had his eyes on the jury as well. It was part of his regular duty to see that the names received by the Sheriff from the Aldermen and City Clerk should contain a fair sprinkling of his friends. In this particular instance he was greatly delighted to notice three of his chums on the panel. It would require much skill and a large supply of eloquence to overcome that impregnable defence, which consisted of Barney and his two adjutants, the member of many years standing in the Massachusetts Medical Society, and the three jurymen. What could break down such a defence?

Having nodded to the crier to announce that the court was open, Judge Patchen busied himself with answering his correspondence. The lawyers occasionally wrangled over some very immaterial matter and called in his Honor to settle the dispute. Other than this, the Judge apparently paid very little attention to what was going on about him. When a new witness came on the stand he would cast a quick glance at him, scratch his name down in a large note book, and then get thoroughly engrossed in his correspondence. When Mrs. Darby took the stand he looked at her a little longer than was his custom with most witnesses, and he thought the face had something familiar about it, which interested him.

"Where have I seen those eyes before"? he thought, and then recalling the night in Pop's sanctum, "Oh! Yes, Madge Styles," and he laughed to himself and went on with his correspondence.

The case for the plaintiff was not long in going in. It was that Mrs. Darby, one afternoon in July, was alighting from a car on Tremont street, when the conductor carelessly sounded the bell, the car started up, and poor Mrs. Darby was thrown violently to the pave-

ment and unceremoniously tumbled about.
Three or four black-and-blue marks on the
back for many days had indicated the nature
of her injury and what might be expected to
follow as a natural sequence, irritation of the
spine and nervous shock.   This seemed pretty
plain sailing; but when the medical expert began to dilate on "contusions" and "extravasa-
tions," the case assumed at once a very deep
and complex character.   The many business
engagements of this gentleman were such that
his evidence was allowed to go in out of the
usual order.   Poor Mrs. Darby sat down at
Pop's side as she listened to what was intended
to prejudice the jury against the truth of her
previously given testimony.   Her face paled,
and the large liquid black eyes were more
prominent than ever.   She placed her hands
on her attorney's shoulder and whispered:

"Oh! Mr. Ormond, how can he say what he
does!   Has he never known the reality of nervous suffering?   I may be nervous, but it's
real to me"!

Shocked as she was at the gentlemanly expert's diagnosis and prognosis, it was as nothing
to her indignation on listening to the story of
the undertaker's adjutants.

"O, Mr. Ormond, why do they allow such
things?   That witness, when he says I tripped
on my dress, must know it's a lie."

"Don't be alarmed, my good woman," Pop said in a whisper. "Don't be alarmed; this fellow is lying, and I shall catch him. It will help our case." And so it did. For when Pop began his cross-examination, he walked in front of the liar, and in a pleasant, conversational tone enquired if the story he had just told was precisely the story Barney Garraghan had told him to tell, and the witness, not seeing the trap, answered quickly :—

" Yes, sorr, precisely the same."

And everybody, including the judge and jurors, laughed.

" I think you may leave the stand," said Pop.

And he did, looking ashamed and bewildered. The effect of this on his partner was such that his evidence was given in a very hesitating manner, and all his statements were so qualified that the impression produced was not particularly strengthening to the defendant's case.

Then, of course, the attorneys on either side summed up in the usual fashion.

The attorney for the corporation followed the rule ordinarily adopted in such cases. He was very calm in his manner, very precise in his diction, and took the jury into his confidence. He dilated on the too frequent assaults on corporations in cases of this kind, and showed the jury how the orphans and widows who were stockholders in the railway suffered in the reduction of their income by reason of the cruel and unjust verdicts that the corporations were obliged to meet.' He urged the jury to carefully consider the evidence of so honest and beloved a physician as the expert was, which must certainly convince the jury that the plaintiff was shamming as regards her injuries, and begged for a verdict for the defendant at their hands.

And Pop told them of the sufferings of his client, how she could never come into court again and ask for further damages, how the sum awarded now must compensate her for her injuries for all time, how the expert was simply a professional witness hired many times every year for just this purpose, and then held up to ridicule the evidence of Barney's adjutants.

And then Judge Patchen, looking extremely bored and somewhat irritated at being obliged to leave his correspondence unfinished, informed the jury of the law governing such cases and impressed them with the fact that the plaintiff must satisfy them of her good faith, and inasmuch as the medical expert's evidence had been uncontradicted and unshaken, they should carefully consider whether the plaintiff had really been injured at all.

At this the black eyes of Mrs. Darby flamed with fire. Unable to control herself, she broke out in a voice that must have been audible to

other ears than those of her attorney, for whom
they were meant : —

"And *he* condemns me. *He* of all men!
He says that I have not suffered. He! My
God, is this the recompense awarded me. and
after all these years! Has he forgotten"? But
Pop checked her, and she drew back in her
chair, her handkerchief covering the glistening
eyes, the lashes of which were now wet with
tears. Though he stilled her further utterance
then, he could not restrain his client from
leaving the court room and following the justice,
who marched towards his lobby with a sheriff
attendant. The Judge was entering his room,'
leading from the passageway, when he felt a
hand upon his arm.

"You, too, say I shammed! *You* say it! The
lines on my face are not indeed caused by this
injury. They were left there many years ago
by the forgetfulness of one who promised, Oh,
how faithfully! Do *you* remember it, Col.
Lawrence? Do *you* remember it? Look,
then "! and stretching out her hand she showed
him the keepsake he had given Madge Styles.
The deputy sheriff waved his hand, tried to
push her aside with a " be off, be off, you must
not stay here."

"Does *he* tell me to go "? pointing to the
Judge, who, flushed and trembling, stood silent.

"Does *he* tell me to go "?

There was no answer, only a slight motion to the officer to leave them. They stood alone in the deserted passageway, those two. The past rose before him. The one woman of his early choice at his side. Neither spoke. Each was mentally turning over the placid, happy hours in old Annecy. For a moment neither stirred. Then she asked:

"And so *you* say I am shamming under my oath *now*, as you shammed in your pledged love then"?

She gazed on him. He, not able to bear the glance of those eyes, looked on the floor, and then in broken tones muttered:

"Marie, forgive. I am an equal sufferer. You shall hear from me soon, elsewhere than here. Not now, not here. Forgive." And he passed into the room and gently closed the door, leaving her alone in the passageway, save only for Pop, who had hurried from the court room to find her.

Pop and his client moved silently through the passageway into the hallway and then out of the hallway from the Court House into the street. Neither made reference to the interview just narrated. Pop wondered what it all meant. Marie Darby thought — Ah! what did she think! The verdict, what it might be, did not concern her now. The past had swallowed up the present. In memory she lived again

through all the swiftly-fleeting dreams of love
and hope of many years ago that had been so
sadly blasted. Pop went to his office. She,
not wishing to wait to hear the verdict, went to
her home, asking that the result might be com-
municated to her when the jury had arrived at
a decision. Barney Garraghan whistled to
himself as he hurried by them on his way to
the office of Mr. Nicholas Nathaniel Nutbourne, the boss. Once in the building it was
easy enough for even the uninitiated to find
the office of this magnate, for the way to it had
been so defaced by tobacco juice and cigar
stubs, so thoroughly blackened by the slush
and mud of these many years that had been
macerated and ground into the floor by the
tread of manifold heelers, that even after the
hall had been swept and cleaned by the janitor
there still remained a dark-brown path about
three feet wide, leading from the head of the
stairway to the office of this modern Napoleon,
that reminded one of a running track in a
gymnasium. When Barney entered, he nodded
in a friendly way to the many officials who
occupied the room. The " boss " himself was
not present. Nothing about the room indicated
the nature of the business calling of the proprietor, unless it was a large map of the
city hanging on the walls, which map
showed the various divisions into wards and

precincts. There was no furniture other
than a small roll-top desk, a safe, and
a motley collection of chairs, most of them
at this time occupied by politicians awaiting
the arrival of the boss. Among the crowd
were a number of aldermen of long standing,
and it may incidentally be remarked, therefore,
of bad standing,—an alderman's honesty being
generally in the inverse ratio to his length of
service. First there was the "cement" alderman. His political duty consisted in simply
seeing that all contracts for cement in the various departments went to a single firm with
whom he had friendly relations. To do this
safely and successfully required an intimate
friendship with all the heads of departments
and their purchasing agents. Of course the
cement furnished the city was at top-notch
prices (billed extra Portland cement), while the
quality, well, there's where the "velvet came
in." No matter if any one else offered a much
better grade of cement, capable of standing a
higher test, at a greatly reduced price, it was
never bought. And so, after a while, no one
ever dreamed of selling any cement to the city.
The other dealers in that article knew they
must wait for the death of this particular
cement alderman before any chance of compe-
tition would exist. So they became resigned
to their fate. It should not be presumed for a

moment by the unthinking that there existed
any improper bargain between this favored
cement firm and the cement alderman. The
cementing of their friendship was merely a
coincidence. To presume otherwise would be
an affront to the stainless honor of the alderman in question, who merited and sought only
the applause of virtuous citizens, and was satisfied with the consciousness of his own immacu-
late probity.

Also present on this occasion was the " land "
alderman. His particular political facility lay
in acquiring, by reason of his familiarity with
street, park, and water commissioners, early
information as to what lands the city would
appropriate in the exercise of the right of eminent domain, bonding the same to his under-
strappers at a rate never exceeding the assessed
value, and then disposing of it to the city at
twice or treble the purchase price. He also
represented in the board the business interests
of a large real estate speculator, who was continually purchasing vast areas of land in the
outlying wards, and benefiting by the building
of new streets through his possessions at the
expense of the city, all this being accomplished
by the far-seeing efforts of the aforesaid " land "
alderman. This the speculator paid for during
the city campaigns by issuing circulars to his
many business and social friends, urging the

duty of electing the "land" alderman, who
alone could properly guard the interests of all
honest citizens and destroy the supremacy of
the rule of the ring.

Seated in a rocking-chair, looking like a new-
born babe, beemed the "oil" alderman, who
did the same for oils that the first-named alderman did for cement, the great concern which
he represented billing to him at twelve and a
half cents what was sold to the city for thirty.
To assume that the difference between twelve
and a half cents and thirty cents represented a
commission to him would be beyond the possi-
bilities of belief, seeing he was such a good
fellow and so inspired with lofty ideals of duties
to his fellow-man. The particular way in which
these "commodity" aldermen worked was to
"hold up" nominations for heads of departments until a proper understanding was had as
to purchases in the future, when confirmation
quickly took place.

Another official of paramount importance to
the well ordering of the city affairs was the
"Steamer," so called. His special duty was to
open sealed bids, by holding the envelope over
escaping steam, and thus learning the nature
of the several bids and conveying the intelligence to the proper alderman, representing
"cement," "land," "oil," "coal," "iron," "lum-
ber," "patents," "provisions," and whatsoever
article of which the city had need.

Then there was the "ballot" alderman, who was always appointed to a place on the committee to recount contested election, being selected for his well-known capacity to count the ballots his way. A most useful and necessary official. In different parts of the room, huddled together, were a large number of contractors, political chairmen of ward committees, "healers," "thugs," "bums," repeaters and ballot box-stuffers. They smoked, chewed, expectorated and argued while they anticipated the coming of the boss. It was the epitome of municipal control in an educated and flourishing city, the ripe fruit of the Puritan representative government for, of and by the people, whereby the servants chosen by the people employ their time in so administering affairs that the city shall pay extortionate prices for all it requires, and the taxes of the inhabitants be proportionately increased,—an institution in which the servants throttle the masters,—the sarcasm of free government, the irony of blackmail. Barney's coming was a pleasurable incident. They all knew it meant business. That the boss had summoned *him* indicated something important was about to be executed. The "grave yard undertaker" was known to all politicians, his wares were always in demand. Barney had hardly gone the rounds of the various visitors, shaking this one by the hand, enquiring of that one as to his "best health," and also venturing his opinion that he knew they were all solid with the boss, when the door opened and Nicholas Nathaniel Nutbourne entered. He was accompanied by his man Friday. This man Friday was the inseparable companion of the boss and always executed his orders with unflinching courage and marked dispatch. His special duty was to circulate and magnify, when he could, the various scandals and lies that the boss wished put in circulation. Though the language used by the boss in these pretended statements of fact was not of the choicest kind, his man Friday, before giving them currency, always endeavored to intersperse them with coarse epithets and oaths, which he apparently considered as imparting to them an added virility and veracity. Before Mr. Nicholas Nathaniel Nutbourne could seat himself at his desk, the door of the office opened and vigorous applause greeted the appearance of a new comer. The caller was a most venerable and benevolent looking individual, resembling in appearance William Penn or other Quaker apostle. A calm, benignant radiance emanated from his whole being, which seemed entirely out of place in such a company, but politics makes strange bedfellows. This man was known as the "Bleacher." Possessed of much informa-

tion and a facile pen, he was particularly happy
in practising the art of whitewashing
black records, and hence the soubriquet of
" Bleacher." Few records so black but that
his genius could made them white as driven
snow; and when too black to be so treated,
the " Bleacher" overcame the difficulty by
stoutly asserting that no such record existed,
or that the truth of it had long since been dis-
proved and did not require his attention. Mr.
Whitebad, for that was his name, smiled benef-
icently at his reception, and casting a fatherly
glance about the assembly, seated his idyllic
person on a modest stool in a corner of the
room, and beamed complacently on the boss,
who was now preparing to lay before his friends
and supporters "one of the most important
questions he had ever been called upon to
decide."

CHAPTER IX.

A LESSON IN ENERGY.

Nothing in the personal appearance of Nicholas Nathaniel Nutbourne indicated the possession of abilities commensurate with the power he was credited with possessing or the influence he was supposed to exert, unless it was a sort of indefinable resemblance to the pictures of Napoleon in his youthful days. He was generally spoken of as being "very energetic." Now, in politics, a man of "energy" is first of all one who arrives at his end by means which the respectable citizen shrinks to employ; secondly, the term "energy" is used to designate the power of extracting "boodle," as it is called, from all those who can be compelled to pay it, and that, too, in the largest amount and quickest time. Nutbourne answered both these definitions. Nor is this said in any discrediting sense. His nature was such that it was utterly incomprehensible to him how any one should be in politics except for pecuniary gain, so he could not be blamed for his course. Not suspecting for a moment, such his mental obliquity, that it was not in accordance with the foundation principles of popular

government to stuff the ballot-box, alter the
returns by false counts, levy blackmail on the
gamblers, extort money from the keepers of
disreputable resorts, he never hesitated to employ any and all these methods. Those who
had the rashness to oppose any of his deep-
laid plans were sure to receive the full measure
of obloquy and slander at his hands. In such
a case, Friday was in a state of mental and
moral exaltation, for wherever that worthy went,
whether it was in theatre lobbies or hotel corridors, he repeated the epithets, prefixing each
and every one of them with a mighty oath.
Still the boss was continually increasing his
list of friends and supporters. Precisely why,
no one could explain, unless it was that he was
"good to his friends," as it is called. This
means to look out that "Tom, Dick and Harry,"
who could gather votes for him, should have
valuable contracts at City Hall, or liquor
licenses, or hold some position as an election
officer. It certainly was noticeable that as
soon as one failed in business or lost his job of
work, he became a Nutbourne boomer. Again,
he always had a *clientèle* of rich men who
wanted honorary positions in the political world
and were willing to pay for it. Not understanding the devious ways of politics, and never
having done anything to their fellow-men to
win their affection and regard, it became neces-

sary for these gentlemen to get votes or appoint-
ments through the influence of Nutbourne,
for which they were willing to pay handsomely,
as a matter of business. Ever afterwards
they felt obliged, in order to keep the past
secret, to speak kindly and flatteringly of Mr.
Nutbourne. Hence his supposed influence
with leading business men and their public en-
dorsement of him. The manner in which he
attempted to conciliate his enemies and draw
them to the support of his measures and candidates indicated only ordinary mental processes.
He began with flattery; if that was of no avail,
then he proceeded with dire threats. Failing
to accomplish his end, he then covered his
opponent with foulest slander and epithets of
contempt.

He began in somewhat this fashion : — putting one hand on the shoulder of the patient,
while the other dangled the masonic charm
attached to the watch chain, he said, in a sup-
plicating tone : " Now, I wish you were with
me in this fight, Brown. If I only had you
with me I should n't care who was against
me. I would rather have your influence than
that of any other politician in this city.
I should win out if you only were with me.
Don't you think you can be with me ? I
tell you, Brown, I don't 'forget my friends.'
I could be an awful good friend to you;

we ought to be together." Then, twirling
the masonic charm: "Blood is thicker than
water, Brown; blood is thicker than water."

If all this did n't fetch Brown, then the *torture extraordinaire* was put in force.

Bill McGonigle — Nutbourne's former political tutor — was put to work to ascertain what
skeleton in the closet existed in Brown's past
life; and when some old mistake or error in his
early days had been dug up, it was put in good
shape, and the suggestion conveyed to the hap-
less Brown that unless he supported Nutbourne's candidates this old story would be
revived, and it would probably ruin him with
his employers. If Brown could resist this
threat, he was indeed a hero. If he still declared his faith and refused support to the
Nutbourne *régime*, then this old story was put
into circulation through Friday, with all the
oaths and epithets and foul suggestion that the
combined imagination of Nutbourne, McGonigle and Friday could invent or suggest.

This method of procedure was certainly
worthy of a Napoleon in politics. Nothing
pleased the "boss" so much as to be called the
"Young Corporal" or the "Corsican." He
studied the Napoleon proverbs and fancied he
was carrying out their ideas. As the great
emperor loved to decorate everything with
"N," so Nutbourne felt it was fate that the

first letter of his three names began with " N,'
and he, also, in his idle moments, scrawled the
famous letter over everything.   Napoleon's
saying, " that of the sixty thousand men making
my army at Eylau, some thirty thousand were
thieves and burglars," and his other remark,
" I get many millions by taxing the vices, will
the virtues yield me as much "? — Nutbourne
made his main rule of political conduct.

If there was a police commissioner especially
noted for his " flyness," you might be sure that
Nutbourne cultivated his acquaintance and
gave it out that he controlled him.   Hence all
the gamblers, liquor dealers and proprietors of
illicit resorts enrolled themselves under Nutbourne.   The boss was always on the most
intimate terms with those captains of police
who controlled the various tenderloin districts.
It was easy to understand how he ruled the
nether side of society and fairly represented
the grasping desires of the vicious.   As .the
supporters of Charles I. defended the breach
of his oath of office by pointing to his faithful
adherence to his marriage vows, so the followers of the boss opposed the attacks of his
enemies by the assertion of his domestic con-
tinence.   When any one argued with lovable
Mr. Whitebad about the trickery, knavery and
deceit of Nutbourne, the venerable gentleman
opened his eyes and pleasantly enquired,

"Why, isn't he a good family man"? The friends of Nutbourne always called him "Natty"; his enemies spoke of him as "Old Nick," while dear Deacon Titmouse of the Baptist Church referred to him as "My energetic Saint Nicholas, a veritable Nathaniel, in whom is no guile."

On this particular day the boss had a strained air, and as he swung round in his office chair, bit his thin lips severely as preparatory to the important statement he was about to communicate. And this was the information: "I have called you together to ask your advice. As you all know, I have never held office and never cared for one. I have been content simply to do my duty as a citizen and faithfully serve my friends. Some of my friends have been very importunate in their demand that I should allow my name to go before the convention as a candidate for the mayoralty."

Who the friends were who had insisted on this course he did not state. As his most intimate friends were in that room, it was strange they had not heard of it before. The announcement was received with clapping of hands, stamping ·of feet and loud "Ahs"! "Whews·"! "Hurrahs"! McGarraghan said "Bully," with great vehemence.

"We're all with you, Natty," was uttered by many.

Mr. Whitebad mildly chimed in with an " admirable "!

Serene resignation pervaded the countenance of the aldermen.

" We 'll show 'em how to run a campaign as is a campaign," was the opinion of Friday.

While a number chorused in answer, " you bet."

" I did 'nt know how you 'd all feel," went on the boss, " but now your good-will is perfectly evident, and I shall abide by your decision, much as I dislike the duty you have imposed on me." More vigorous applause.

" The first thing to do is to arrange for calling the caucuses before the close of summer."

"Ah ! dat 's de business," shouted Barney. " Dese silver tops will all be on dere vacation, cutting dere coupons off at Nahant and Newport."

This first piece of advice met with general approval.

The next statement vouchsafed by the boss was to the effect that his warm friend Bill McGonigle would soon return to the city and could be relied on to carry his ward in the convention. The enquiry was then made of Barney to state to the meeting the *modus operandi* adopted by him in his ward with such signal success, hoping it might be of advantage to the others present in formulating plans of procedure in their own caucuses.

"Well, I tells how we do it where I hang out," said the undertaker. "I have a big crowd of my boys on hand in de hallway, and wen dese fellers from the hill goes by 'em dey marks a white chalk cross on dere backs. Den I have a crowd of fellers who knows how to put up dere dukes in de hall, and when doze other fellers gets into line to vote, dey goes in too, and shoves and pushes and crowds 'em out of the line, so dey don't get a chance to vote. If dey objects, why, give it to 'em from the shoulder."

"How about the police, will they allow it"? asked some one.

"Will dey allow it"? said the undertaker scornfully.

"De perlice! I should like to see 'em object. Don't dey owe their persish to me and Mr. Nutbourne? Well, I guess dey don't object. Dey simply tells the silver tops dat the law don't allow 'em to interfere. And dere nibs gits easily discouraged and goes home. Dere's more than one way of skinning a cat, I tells yer! Me ward is all right, and ivery diligate will be for our good friend Nicholas Nathaniel Nutbourne."

This brought out more applause.

The "ballot" alderman told them there was no difficulty in his ward, that the returns would be all right when received, and that he would see to it that he was chairman of his caucus. No one ever accused him of the vote not being as he wanted it. Nearly every ward was heard from and the most satisfactory assurances of success secured. The boss informed his followers that they must get to work at once forming their delegations, and in those wards where opposition might be expected an extra delegation, headed "unpledged," must be put into the caucus. This would draw away from the opposition. In his own ward Mr. Nutbourne had one unfailing method of securing the delegation in his interest. The ticket was always made up of gentlemen of the most unquestioned ability, dignity and character, men who disliked mingling in politics and were strongly averse to attending conventions. Such a ticket was sure of election. After the caucus was over the boss went to the several hightoned delegates and informed them that nothing of importance was to be transacted at the convention and he would endeavor to find a substitute to act for them, and thus relieve them of the disagreeable duty of going to the convention. For which act of courtesy Mr. Nutbourne received profound thanks. The credentials therefore remained in the hands of the boss, who sold them to the highest bidder, or used them in the interests of his friends.

The unanimity of the gathering was such

that the boss felt his presence was no longer
required, and as he was needed elsewhere he
left them in charge of Friday, who, he had no
doubt, would attend to the needful. The
"needful" referred to cigars, a box of which
Friday was opening as Mr. Nutbourne withdrew. The boss hurried on to the police
station in the main tenderloin district, over
which presided his warm friend, Captain
Phillimore.

In order to understand the warmth of the
affection existing between Nutbourne and the
Captain, we must fully comprehend the business
that was regularly transacted within the jurisdiction of that station. In this district flourished
the gamblers and the keepers of disreputable
resorts. These various occupations needed
protection; the public needed their service.
No one could reasonably object, therefore, if
they were allowed to exist, nor should any be
envious if the receipts for protecting this necessary traffic and service was correspondingly
large. The business was conducted in the
most systematic method, at least so far as the
houses of ill repute were concerned. On the
first day of each and every month, payment
ranging from fifteen to thirty dollars a month
was made to the Captain's friend, Isaac Aaronson, an insignificant cigar manufacturer. If
the monthly due was not forthcoming on that

day, Isaac called at the delinquent's house, just
a friendly call, you know. Nothing was said
about the dues, of course. This was hint
number one. If it did not bring immediate
settlement that evening, a police officer casually
dropped in the next day. He simply remarked
on the weather, and carelessly enquired if business was good. This was hint number two. Woe
betide the proprietor who did not take heed of
that terrible warning, for the next night the
house would be "pulled," and its occupants
huddled off to the police station, to be arraigned
in court the following day,— and all in the
name of virtue. In the course of a year the
revenue derived from such source, in a district
where every third building harbored such resorts, was fabulous.

The system had been invented by the boss,
and the Captain had received his appointment
through Natty's "pull" with the commissioners; so Nutbourne received a pretty tidy
"divvy." Whether any of the principal fund
went higher than the Captain, none knew,
many suspected.

The gamblers generally paid the demands
made on them in much larger amounts, though
of less frequent occurrence, to the Captain
directly or to the boss.

The saloons were worked in a wholly different way. They were the joint prey of the

Captain and Isaac Aaronson. When any new saloon was opened, the Captain, in company with Isaac, called on the proprietor, and a conversation something like the following ensued:

"Good stand you have here."

"Tolerably so, Mr. Officer."

"Ought to sell a good many cigars"?

"We hope so."

"My friend, Mr. Aaronson, manufactures capital cigars."

"Ah! Pleased to know Mr. Aaronson."

"If you've not all you want in stock, remember him."

"Should be pleased to buy of any friend of yours, Captain."

"I recommend his wares. Everybody round here buys of him."

"Well, well, I'm glad you spoke of it. I will give him an order now."

"No time like the present. Good day."

The order was given forthwith. The cigars that Isaac concocted were of the poorest quality, while the price was the highest the frequenters of saloons in that neighborhood could afford to pay. And every saloon keeper, no matter how his customers objected to Isaac's wares, was obliged to keep on hand a certain number of boxes and push the sale thereof. If any one failed to come up to the limit fixed by the captain, one of the patrolmen would stroll into such saloon and anxiously enquire what the trouble was between the proprietor and the captain, or " old man," as they generally call him. No further hint was necessary. An extra large order, spot cash, was immediately given. The profits of Aaronson's cigar factory were divided between the captain and Isaac in the proportion of two to one. It can readily be figured that the profits of a captain's position in such a district were not far from what is paid as the salary of the President of these great United States.

Of course Mr. Nutbourne was a welcome visitor. He marched up the steps of the station, swung in behind the rail and seated himself side of the captain with the air of one who owned the whole place. The lieutenant, sergeant and roundsmen all raised their hats to him. The boss then announced to the captain his intention of going for that City Hall, and intimated that if at the end of the year there was anything left of it but the foundation, the citizens were to be congratulated.

" Now, Cap., we've got to rearrange our lines in this ward, and I have a scheme for the suppression of vice " (here he grinned and winked knowingly) "that will keep up the income all the while. Every one knows that you and I are friends, that I really keep you here. They say vice flourishes in this district, and that will be used against me when I am running for the nomination. They'll say I am a dangerous man to put in the mayor's chair, and point to you and the district for proof. We'll meet it in this way. Shut up every house of ill repute in your territory except twenty, and raise the price of protection to each to one hundred dollars per month. They'll pay it eagerly enough, for we guarantee to them that there shall be only twenty in the precinct. So they will get all the business. In the end it's just the same to them. Nay, it's better for them. We get the same revenue at less bother of collecting. And the good people will praise you to the skies for cleaning out the district."

The captain, who had been drinking in every word, leaned back in his chair, slapped "Natty" on the shoulder and laughingly cried out :—

"I'll be d——d, Natty, my boy, if you ain't energetic. It's a great scheme, and we'll work it to the queen's taste. You *have* got energy."

"I'm not through yet," went on the boss, "Aaronson must see all the liquor men in this ward and look to it that when the caucuses come their whole crowd votes here first. Then Johnson's livery stable must furnish barges to take them out to Roxbury and Dorchester, where Barney Garraghan will tell them what tickets to vote there. Now, there are two independent leaders who live in this ward,

Larry O'Neil and Peter Fitzgerald. They must be got hold of. They are kickers, but they both want a license. You see them and tell them that I 'll guarantee them a license from the commissioners."

"You can get it for them if anybody in this city can," broke in the Captain.

" Well, they know that. Only they will have to promise to buy their beer from Gilroy's brewery, mind that. Now, I must go. There 's a fellow over in East Boston who 's got a big pull there, whose brother is to be sentenced in court this afternoon, and I have promised that I will have one of the commissioners lay down on the judge, who 's a friend of his, to put the case on file. Now hustle." And he trotted out of the office and skipped down the steps, the captain watching him, as he went, with fond admiration, and muttering to himself, " what energy ! what energy !"

CHAPTER X.

THE SKELETON IN THE CLOSET.

It is hardly necessary to observe that the verdict in Mrs. Darby's action was far from satisfactory to her attorney. Pop was seated at his desk when the messenger brought him the information that the jury had come in. It was late in the afternoon, and the Judge had kept the court open longer than usual, waiting for the return of the jury. The verdict was for the plaintiff, to be sure, but then the amount was disappointing. To let Mrs. Darby know was a question with him. He was turning the matter over in his mind when who should enter but Judge Patchen. He motioned to Pop to go into the growlery, where he had first met Madge Styles and given her the fatal pocket-piece.

"My dear Ormond, I come to make a confession. I come to reveal what I supposed was forever hidden and buried. But you saw enough to-day to know that my duty is to tell you all and let you know what I purpose doing." Pop bowed and listened, his eyes never leaving those of the Judge. The Jurist went on:

"When I was a young man, in the flush of youth, I accompanied my uncle to the baths at

Aix-les-Bains. It was only a short distance from there to old Annecy. I often went there with an English cavalry officer, then at Aix-les-Bains for treatment. At Annecy I met Marie Rouband, a beautiful French girl about twenty years of age. I was introduced to her as Colonel Lawrence, an assumed name, of the American army. I need not say I fell desperately in love. All that summer I saw her nearly every day. Together we climbed those purple hills, strolled through the emerald fields and sailed the peaceful lake that adds the loveliness of Como to the grandeur of Leman. She had beauty, intelligence, character, in fullest measure. Oh! What Elysian days those were! At last autumn came. What divine hours those were! Where else does nature seem to die, like youth and beauty, in all its grace and serenity. The very air and scenery were made for love. I plighted mine and she returned the promise of my faith. When the time came for my uncle's departure, I promised her to return to France shortly and make her my wife, and she gave me that pocket-piece as token of her trust, which I had carried ever since till that night I gave it to her daughter, Madge Styles.

"My uncle's health did not improve, and when America was reached he was a very sick man. On our arrival in New York we learned of the

failure of my father's house. I was penniless.
My uncle shortly afterwards became a hopeless
invalid. My marriage with the lady who became my wife was most desired on his part;
she had wealth and position; I had neither,
then. Pop, I forgot the pledge I made abroad.
I broke my word to Marie Rouband. I did as
my uncle desired — I married; he died shortly
and left me what fortune he possessed. Of
course I never heard from France. My name
there was Colonel Lawrence. No letters, if any
such were ever sent me, reached me. Time
went on. I buried myself in the law. Hearing
nothing after many years, I naturally supposed
the object of my first love had died, or perhaps
had gone her way and married some one else.
I ceased to think of her. My work, my cares,
my labors consumed all my thoughts. Then
came my appointment to the bench. I em-
braced the opportunity to still further occupy
my thoughts. My wife died. She had no
children. Day and night I devoted to my
new duties, and these many years have seen
me constant in my work. The dreams of old
Annecy, that broken vow, the one shadow of
my existence, rarely now disturbed me.

"What a cruel effacer is time"! A long pause
ensued. Then the Judge arose. "Pop, so far
as it rests in my power, I mean to mend the
wrong I committed in my early days; I shall

make you my almoner. I will not make my-self further known to your client other than to execute to you a deed of trust of property sufficient to yield her an ample income for her life. You shall prepare the deed. I will sign most gladly. I do it willingly and with the hope it may in part palliate my wrong. Do not tell her of this paltry verdict of the jury; but let her know the rest at once, and ease her mind. While I live she shall never suffer."

The tears rolled down his cheek. Pop grasped his hand. Their eyes met and both were wet with tears. The verdict was forgot-ten. As the Judge passed out of the office into the hallway, Pop mused: "So the Judge has a skeleton in his closet after all. Life is the same everywhere."

CHAPTER XI.

A STRONG MAN.

Some weeks after the event narrated in the last chapter, Pop sat in the library of Bulrush Morgan, awaiting the coming of that prominent and respectable capitalist. His eyes wandered over the various shelves, filled with costly tomes bound in fancy colors as if to match the costumes worn by their owner. Mr. Morgan evidently liked the looks of the outside of his books even if he was not acquainted with the inside. "I would n't know all that is inside of these books for a fortune. How it must cumber the mind and prevent its action," thought Pop. "The regular books of reference, the regular treatises on philosophy, the approved works of history, the proper English novels. I wonder can they teach a man anything? All correct. All in their proper order. Probably bought by the entire job. Why does a man whose life is grounded in pork want to be considered bookish? Can he ever remove the taint"? The more Pop thought it over, the more indignant he became, until, when Mr. Morgan arrived, he was fairly boiling, and, without any words of greeting, addressed him brusquely with, —

"Will you tell me the reason why you bought all those lying volumes called 'histories'"?

Mr. Morgan stared at him. Then, reddening and looking somewhat confused, remarked:

"Why, why, don't a man want to know what his fellow-man has done in the past? Can he not guide himself more correctly by learning what has happened as a result of certain principles"?

"Precisely, you put it well enough, only you assume your premises without enquiring whether they be correct. History, we are told, is simply philosophy teaching by example. But if the example stated is untrue, pray tell me how the deductions therefrom can be correct? This history business is a profound lie. Napoleon understood that when he said history was an agreed fable. So it is, nothing more. Therefore you can deduce nothing from it. It is simply a humbug, a lie. Take your own history. Take the Revolution and Independence. We teach the boys and girls at schools that it was a struggle on the principle that taxation without representation is tyranny; but you and I know it all grew out of John Hancock's rum. Now why not be honest and tell the children the facts? Oh, no; oh, no, that would not be moral. So we put it on a high ground that never existed. Take another case, take your United States Constitution, about which so many good things are said. I know, as an attorney, that there was no great moral or intellectual mystery about it. It was simply a trade compact. Nothing more, nothing less. Why, the only vitality to it, that has kept the breath in its body, is the 'commerce clause.' Rhode Island at first would n't join the Union, because she thought she had the greatest port in America and wanted to hog the trade. What did she want of a trade compact that gave every one the right to use that port, her only asset? Your government is founded on trade, common, coarse trade. Your constitution resulted from nothing else, notwithstanding its glittering preamble. You don't teach the scholars that. You make up a wholly different story and make them swallow it. So it is through all time. Man is so ashamed of his work that he does not dare to tell the truth about it. The church has done the same by the middle ages. History is a cunningly devised lie."

Morgan had recovered his equinimity and suggested it was a pity that the world at large did not agree with Mr. Ormond.

"Well," replied Pop, "let's take a case in point. Were you called upon some years hence to write the history of the Metropolitan Water Supply Co., think you you would

relate the real details of its birth, the peculiar
travail it underwent during its incubation in
the Legislature? Not much. There would not
be the suspicion of the use of money. It would
all be principle and wisdom on the part of the
far-seeing legislators. It would not be of any
use to another generation who sought to
ascertain the manner of passing such legislation
at this time."

The mention of Mr. Morgan's experience
with the cheerful Massachusetts Legislature
caused him to smile, and forced him to admit
that perhaps there might be some truth in what
Pop had suggested.

"I tell you what I say is absolutely true.
We are told that 'Nature admits no lie.' But
the fact is she invents them constantly. Everywhere it is lie, lie, lie. The colors we see, the
sounds we hear do not exist in the things
themselves, they are in us. Our senses are
always deceiving us. The object of life is to
teach us not to believe what we see, hear,
touch, feel, or think. The only difference between the savage and the civilized man rests
in the fact one trusts his senses and the other
does not."

Having blown himself off, and taken to himself one of Morgan's prime cigars, Pop said he
was now prepared to listen, and hoped he had
not interfered with any matter Mr. Morgan
wished to lay before him.

Mr. Nutbourne's campaign to capture the Republican nomination had not met with favor in certain quarters. But he was "hustling" at so lively a rate and making adherents every day, that those citizens who were opposed to the man and his methods were anxiously casting about for a candidate who was strong enough to beat him. Such a one was difficult to find, for no one desired entering the lists with the boss. His power of slander was well known and deterred most any one from fighting him. A strong man was needed, but difficult to find. A strong man by no means indicates one possessed of strong mental or moral qualifications. The term refers to one who can get votes and have the "boys" and "heelers" with him, one who is not afraid to tap the barrel freely and often.

Morgan's legislative campaign in the matter of the Metropolitan Water Supply Co. had met the full anticipations of the leg pullers, and this, coupled with the success attained, made him a strong man. The opponents of Nutbourne turned to him at this juncture as the one man who could save them and scatter the forces of the boss ; and it was with reference to his becoming a candidate that Mr. Morgan had asked Pop to call on him for the purpose of consultation. Pop gave him the same advice that every one else had done.

"Run by all means if you desire the nomination, for you can certainly get it. Only remember one thing, you must expect the foulest calumny to be heaped upon you by the boss and his satellites. The most outrageous slanders will be invented and you will be accused of perpetrating offences you never dreamed of committing."

"That does not trouble me. Leg pulling is the only thing to which I do seriously object, and I think you will admit I have made full proof of my ministry in that regard. Pop, I mean to show these pure-bred Bostonians what cowards they are to be afraid of this foul-mouthed blackguard of a Nutbourne. He's been working at it for many weeks, and even claims now that he is a sure winner with a majority of the wards at his back, but he's a blower, and what he claims is false. I've met just such fellows as he in the mines and slums of the west. They don't frighten me, only, in Heaven's name, deliver me from the New England leg puller, that's the only fellow I flee from. I know where this Nutbourne's strength is,— in the tenderloin district and in the rum wards,— but I'll lead him a lively chase there. This man's weapons are dangerous, but the only thing he fears is money, for he knows that will take his vicious supporters away from him. Now I shall want advice as I go along, and how much will you want as a retainer"?

When Pop answered "Nothing," Morgan started and looked incredulously at him.

"No," said Pop, "I never take money from any friend (and I take the liberty of considering you such) for service in his behalf when he is a candidate for office. My time and ability from now to the election are at your command."

Morgan had been so long in the habit of paying for everything he received in this world that he could hardly believe his senses. Finally he remarked:

"Well, I do want your services, and I do want to remunerate you, but if you say you won't let me do so, why I suppose I must remain your debtor."

As regards the campaign, both were wrong and both were right. The boss took pains that the slanders should be of such devilish character as to cause the most exquisite suffering to Morgan, though he boasted his indifference to abuse. Besides, there was more leg pulling, and Mr. Morgan was caused to bleed again. He was right in his view that the blackleg supporters of Nutbourne would yield to dollars, for he bought his chosen henchman right away from him. But, before he received the nomination, Morgan had to travel a pretty thorny path and entertain new experiences in politics besides leg pulling.

The announcement that Justin Bulrush Morgan would be a candidate awoke the gravest ap-
prehensions in the mind of Nicholas Nathaniel
Nutbourne.   He recognized the power of his
antagonist, a man whose money would offset
the attractions of liquor licenses and police
protection in a very considerable degree.   So
the boss set his wits at work to consider the
best method of besmirching the "strong
man" of the party.   McGonigle, who had now
returned home from his dipsatorial interim,
was at once set at work on the case.   The
past history of Mr. Morgan must be thoroughly
investigated and the least circumstance that
could be blown into a flame to wither and destroy his reputation must be dug up.   In the
meantime Barney Garraghan and his confeder-
ates were to watch the rum shops carefully and
see that no one was allowed to influence the
proprietors.   The police and the fire department were to be thoroughly lobbied, while the
street department and the contractors were to
organize their forces and keep the laborers
from outside pressure.   As the time set for
the caucuses drew near the excitement in both
the parties was at fever heat.   For while Nutbourne continually prated about his thorough
allegiance to the Republican party, he had never
been able to control a caucus of his own faith
except through the introduction of Democrats

to such meetings. When a division of wards
was contemplated, he always arranged the
gerrymander in such a manner as to leave in
every Republican ward at least one precinct
which was thoroughly Democratic, from which
precinct he drafted a large army to manipulate
the Republican nomination. It was the perfecting of this plan that gave him in the present
campaign a remarkable advantage. In addition to this scheme he organized a stevedore
gang from East Boston and a gas-house contingent from the North End. These, together
with the famous band of Roxbury "repeaters"
and peninsular "travellers," made an organization which could compass at least five wards,
voting in each caucus. All these elements
acting in conjunction with the "undertaker's
grave yard" regiment could in ordinary instances control the nominations to any convention.
The boss was confident; but Pop determined
to defeat him on the repeater business. Whatever is done to organize repeating gangs is
always accomplished by night. Such dark
deeds are never done in the light. When the
gas-house laborer or street digger gets through
his day's work, and has his supper, he repairs
to some favorite gin-mill, where an agent of the
boss is on hand, recruiting the forces of his
master. Pop took pains to have a spy in all
such resorts who would keep him informed as

to the rendezvous appointed for each gang on
the night of the caucus. So that when that
night came a detective was present to warn the
would-be Republican caucus packers that their
"jig" was up and they better not disobey
the law. Also, in every caucus where such
"packing" was proposed, Pop had a coura-
geous lieutenant to challenge such voters. In
this way the boss was somewhat disappointed
as to results, and on the morning following the
caucuses the press announced a very close
canvass and intimated great uncertainty as to
the outcome of the convention. The boss
maintained a chipper air and told every one he
was a sure winner. Perhaps he had in mind
the charge he was soon to launch through the
public press regarding serious offences committed by Mr. Morgan some years back, which
charges would be of so damaging a character
as to effectually disqualify Mr. Morgan as a
candidate before the municipal convention.
McGonigle had ascertained that some twenty
or thirty years back the cashier of a large cattle
concern in Missouri had been indicted and con-
victed of embezzlement. To be sure the man
had afterwards been pardoned. And further-
more the convict's name was Morgan. Further
investigation revealed the fact that the criminal was not Justin Bulrush Morgan, but his
brother, who after his release from the peniten-

tiary had moved westward, gone into the
mines and died a millionaire, leaving two
daughters. These daughters were now visit-
ing at Mr. Morgan's house, one of them only
recently engaged to a distinguished descendant
of one of the Pilgrim fathers. As the boss
listened to these incidents, his cold eye sparkled
and his whole presence became radiant. He
would charge the crime on Morgan. How
easy to insinuate that Morgan, the pork
packer, was engaged by the aforesaid cattle
firm, had betrayed the trust, had been indicted,
was a felon! Ought now to be occupying a
felon's cell rather than the position of a candidate for mayor of the noblest municipality on
earth! Neither would Morgan dare to deny
the charge. To do that would be only to
expose his own brother's rascality and blight
the future of those young girls, who as yet had
never heard of their father's wrong. No, Morgan was a man of chivalrous nature. The boss
counted on that. Rather than show his inno-
cence by proclaiming his brother's crime, Morgan would shield his nieces from ignominy and
sorrow, though in silence he himself suffered
the cruelest of torture. The boss knew he had
Morgan in his grasp now surely. On the Sunday preceding the convention the papers should
publish the story, which should simply be the
general rumors to that effect which floated

through cafés and theatre lobbies on the preceding evening, and which had been deftly
wafted everywhere by the loving breath of
Friday.

When the boss revealed to Friday the work
that had been laid out for him, that worthy em-
braced the opportunities now offered to distinguish himself, with unmistakable glee. And
when the boss, exulting, exclaimed, " Now we 'll
stick pins in that ' strong man ' Morgan," Friday
immediately appropriated the phrase and added
to it by indicating in what portion of the human
body the belligerent end of the pins were to be
imbedded. And they did stick pins in him.
And they were sharp ones at that, veritable
stilettos. They went deep into the victim's
soul. The toreadors looked on and enjoyed the
sport. The great strong animal might fret and
fume and bellow and charge, but McGonigle,
the boss, and Friday were safe from his attacks.

CHAPTER XII.

A STUDY IN TREACHERY.

It was Saturday evening preceding the Tuesday on which the convention was holden, that Mr. Morgan felt he was entitled to some recreation to mitigate the asperities of the campaign. He had therefore prepared a theatre party for his daughters and nieces, and some of their young friends. If the young people enjoyed the show, Morgan himself was sure to. His youth had been hard enough, and he tried to throw about his family and friends what enjoyment lay within his power. Not so with the boss and his man Friday. That watchful pair had no time for recreation. They neither slumbered nor slept. Friday started early in the evening on his pilgrimage of slander. He took in the main restaurants about dinner time, from six o'clock to half after seven; and then paid his attention to the theatre lobbies, finally winding up with the after-theatre parties at the various saloons and cafés.

Wherever he appeared he looked lugubrious, was evidently weighed down by some weighty sorrow, bowed solemnly to all who noticed him. Occasionally drew a friend (if his acquaintances could properly be called friends)

aside, and, in a low whisper, as if he feared
some one might overhear him, revealed the
secret, not to be repeated for the world, of
Morgan's false early life. He told his startled
listener how sorry he was for Morgan, that he
feared some newspaper reporter might get
hold of the story; it would hurt the party for so
prominent a man as Morgan to have such a
rumor afloat; would it not be wise for Mr. Morgan's friends to withdraw his candidacy before
it was too late, and so forth and so on. Where
he was sure of his company he did not hesitate
to express his delight and refer to Morgan in
terms of derision and contempt. Before midnight the tale had been given a pretty wide
circulation. The newspaper offices all had it.
The reporters were sent to Mr. Morgan's house
to call his attention to the rumor, and ask
what he wished to say in reply.

So that when Mr. Morgan's carriage drove
up after the theatre was over it was besieged,
and he and the ladies had some difficulty in
making their way up the stone steps to the
vestibule. The ladies entered the house and
Morgan stood on the upper step while one of
the more persistent reporters explained to him
the rumors which were flying thick and fast
through the city, and requested his answer to
the same. A shadow passed across his countenance. He had been having a charming

evening, and all that happiness was to be oblit-
erated now. If he denied that he was the
Morgan mentioned in the serious charge, then
enquiries would be made as to what Morgan it
was, his brother's memory would be blackened,
and the young girls who had just passed within
the door would have their present and future,
perhaps, blasted. If he admitted he was the
Morgan, then he must certainly lose the nomination. And yet there was no time for consideration. The stoop was crowded with reporters. They were hungry for a reply of some
kind. To hesitate was a mistake; to speak
might be ruin. The reporters were beginning
to draw nearer to him and gaze at him more
intently. He could hear within the laughter
and singing of his daughters and nieces. He
felt his heart beating faster. He saw the
mayoralty fading from his grasp. All the while
the wolfish reporters were coming up the steps
and were now close at hand. But politics has
its advantages. It teaches many things; it had
taught Mr. Morgan control. Whatever the
situation, he had learned not to exhibit outward
annoyance, he made "no waves." So, looking
smilingly on the crowd and jingling his keys at
the same time, he jocosely remarked:

"Well, well, they have kept that story back
till pretty late in the campaign, have n't they?
I supposed it would get out long before this.

I sent the associated press full particulars of all these facts three weeks ago, when I consented to become a candidate, and if any newspaper now turns my information against me, without giving my full explanation of the circumstances, I will sue that paper for heavy damages in libel. Good-night, boys. I am sorry you haven't something fresher to give the world." He closed the door quickly and left the somewhat confused reporters on the door stoop, not knowing exactly what course to pursue. As a matter of fact, the Sunday newspapers thought it best not to publish the story, but that made little difference. It had gone abroad and was discussed at church, in the clubs, in fact everywhere. It was having a very appreciable effect on Mr. Morgan's campaign. Here and there a delegate dropped out of the ranks and the line was beginning to waver. It was said that Morgan had had an attack of nervous prostration, and well he might. Nothing had ever stabbed him so deeply as that story, given by McGonigle to the boss, and by the boss to his man Friday, and by Friday to the world. Still, who invented or spread it, he did not know at that time. It was enough that the rumor existed. Would that he had never entered politics! Why should he not have been satisfied with his home, his family, his friends, his wealth? Why

seek to be a public servant? Why try to be
of service to his fellow-man when that fellow-
man would soon despise it!

Saturday night he did not sleep, nor Sunday,
nor Sunday night. He jumped from his
uneasy bed Monday at dawn, brought his fist
down upon the marble slab of the commode,
and with a big, brave oath, swore he would
beat the rascals who had spread that story, and
win the nomination, cost what it might. He
would ask no advice from any one. He would
strike this man Nutbourne in as vital a part as
he himself had been struck. He would send
for the boss' friend and henchman, McGonigle,
and buy him and all he controlled in that
convention. He would let Nutbourne know
the beauties of treachery. With caution,
with precision, he took every step, so there
were no obstacles to the final consummation
of his plan. On the night of the convention, when Pop called to receive his final
advices from Mr. Morgan, he thought he noticed
a vast change in the man. The smile had gone
from his face. Instead there was a determined,
dogged air about the man. Those expressionless eyes seemed to have gathered fire, or was
it blood? The hair seemed to be streaked
with gray, the beard more wiry and unkempt.
The hands were clenched and thrust deep into
the trousers' pockets as if to hide them, else

they betray the commotion that had been going on within. The greeting was hardly cordial, though frank as ever.

"I wanted you, Pop. It's well you're here. I will put some courage in you. We shall win to-night. I am elected on the first ballot; if only you take pains that the counting committee have courage to prevent an illegal ballot."

"I should like nothing better than to see you chosen, but really, Mr. Morgan, you must not be deceived. You are practically defeated now, I fear. That cursed rumor has lost you votes and weakened the *esprit de corps* of your followers," said Pop gently.

"It has, hey, you say it has"? He spoke excitedly, and then calmly said, "Pop, I have bought Bill McGonigle, and to-night pay him the price of nine other delegates he controls. The credentials of five of that number I hold in my hand now," and he threw them on the table.

Pop looked at the credentials with evident pleasure. Mr. Morgan neither smiled or expressed gratification. His face was that of a determined man, one thoroughly in earnest, one bent on some deep and justifiable revenge.

"You are to take these credentials, they cost a good deal more than their weight in gold, and have them voted on by proper parties. As regards the others, McGonigle will furnish the substitutes. He has been well paid for it, and more is to come. He will probably address the convention in Nutbourne's behalf, but he and his gang will vote for *me*. It's most time for the convention to assemble; you'd better go. Much depends on you." As he said this, he spoke slowly and coldly, had perfect command of himself and exerted a marked control over others, for Pop obeyed him like a child, simply suggesting, " Where will you be, so I can let you know the result of the balloting "? Morgan's usually pleasant manner had forsaken him, and he turned disdainfully on the departing attorney, remarking in icy tones :

" I know already what the balloting will show." And very probably he did.

The hall was rapidly filling as Pop entered. He was the centre for Morgan's friends, who eagerly enquired after the health of their candidate, and his chances for success. Knowing what he did, Pop was confident, and the Morgan forces exhibited a courage which somewhat surprised the boss.

Mr. Morgan had shown wisdom in selecting McGonigle as the object of his charity. He knew that the boss controlled the city committee and would select the officers and committees of the convention. He knew also that in the pending fight the chairman of the com-

mittee to collect, sort and count the ballots
would probably be McGonigle, and in this he
was not mistaken. The presiding officer of
the convention would be some highly respected
gentleman without force or political influence,
who existed as a politician solely on his past
character; while the secretaries would be
amiable young gentlemen of club connections,
desirous of entering politics and having their
names in the newspapers. The boss, therefore, had arranged to have the chairman and
secretaries of the convention chosen from the
Morgan supporters. The chairman and a
majority of the counting committee were to be
selected from his own followers. Then the
boss could make a great show of his fair play.
He could say :

"See how generous I am. I give the other
side the presiding officer and both secretaries.
As a mere matter of form, I simply ask for a
chairman of one committee "!

But Morgan's forethought had provided that
the chairman of that committee should be under
his absolute control. Of this action of Mr.
Morgan the boss had no suspicion. The fight
was so hot and the lines so closely drawn that
the convention was impatient for a vote and
was not disposed to listen to long speeches,
though Pop did present Mr. Morgan's name,
which was received with marked applause,

while that of the boss provoked the loudest of cheers when brought forward by Mr. Whitebad and seconded by McGonigle. Cheers that were to be but short-lived, and which turned rapidly to oaths and threats when McGonigle, as chairman of the committee to collect, sort and count the ballots, reported the vote, which showed Justin Bulrush Morgan was the choice of the convention by a majority of three votes. The boss, though, was equal to the occasion. He stilled his excited followers with a wave of the hand, and then proceeded to tell the convention that he "was first, last and always a Republican; that he was never known to bolt; that he pledged the nominee his hearty support; and he knew his own followers would do likewise." This called forth tremendous applause and made Barney Garraghan give utterance to the remark:

"Dat 's de kind of Republicans we are."

But many of the more faithful adherents of the boss crowded around him to learn what was the cause of his defeat, and what plans for the future he was perfecting.

"Who is that Ormond, who was putting up the game for this Morgan"? asked a Nutbourne boomer.

"What, that *bastard*"? answered the boss. "He's a stinker. We are on to him, the d——d——. He got $5,000 for his dirty

work.   Don't you suppose I know?   A warm
friend of mine saw the filthy lucre paid him.
I'll fix him before I get through with him."

Although this statement was made from
whole cloth, his followers accepted it as fact.
When Friday had repeated the falsehood several times, the amount alleged as paid to Pop
had risen to $20,000, and before long the sum
had mounted up to $50,000.   Pop having been
disposed of, the followers of Nutbourne now
pressed him for an answer as to what he proposed to do with Morgan in the campaign.

The boss smiled sardonically, "Do with
him?   Why, we'll give it to him in the neck"!

CHAPTER XIII.

CAIN KILLS ABEL.

No sooner had Mr. Miles Mulvenna read in the columns of the Millville *Democrat* that Mr. Justin Bulrush Morgan had been nominated for mayor by the Republicans of Boston, than he started at once for the Hub to get himself retained as a speaker in labor meetings. Mr. Mulvenna prided himself on his ability to induce the knights of labor and kindred organizations to support as their candidate for office men of unquestioned financial responsibility. When he reached the office of the Metropolitan Water Supply Company, he found it besieged by a vast army of heelers, who were intent upon urging on the president of that corporation their respective "pulls" and the value of the various political clubs to which they might belong.

The leg pullers were out in full force. The vultures had smelt their prey. Their victim was undergoing torture at their hands. But Bulrush Morgan had determined to win the battle at all hazards, and so bore their attacks complacently. The barrel was on tap and the flow therefrom free. Even Mulvenna received a cordial welcome, and the bargain was duly made by which he was to make six speeches during the campaign, the payment whereof was to be deferred till the night preceding the election. Morgan had driven a close bargain. Hereafter, if he was obliged to have the services of Mulvenna, he proposed to pay for them only on delivery of the goods.

Another early caller was Mr. Nicholas Nathaniel Nutbourne, who was demure as possible, and who came, so he said, to congratulate Mr. Morgan on his deserved nomination and proffer him his valuable services. He told the nominee how deeply he regretted that any one should have started that uncalled for and cruel story regarding his early life, assured him he never for a moment believed it, and when he heard it was in circulation personally endeavored to suppress it. Nutbourne laid himself out to exhibit his humility, his love for the party, and his earnest desire for Mr. Morgan's triumphant success. He purred like a cat; he fawned like a dog. Nay, more, he almost grovelled at Morgan's feet. So sincere did he appear that Morgan finally came to the conclusion that this energetic man had been foully misrepresented to him, and when he bade him adieu, thanked him cordially for his services and forced upon him several thousand dollars to be used by the boss in the various

channels with which he was familiar and outside of the control of the city committee.

"What a soft kid"! thought Nutbourne.
"Before I get through I will have pulled his
leg for enough to pay all the expenses of my
campaign, get all the information I need as to
what he is doing, and then give it to him in the
neck. The Republican party will soon see the
mistake it made in not nominating me."

The intimacy of Nutbourne and Morgan
caused much perturbation in the minds of Pop
and his friends. They warned Mr. Morgan
that he would be betrayed, that the boss was
cozening him, that old man Whitebad was as
bad as the boss, that it was unfair to the friends
who nominated him to put them in the power
of their enemy; but all to little purpose. The
boss was so gentle, so loving, so flattering, so
fertile in suggestions, that Mr. Morgan was
fairly captivated by his fascinating powers, and
opened his heart and pocket-book to him. So
Pop knew he must rely on his own ability to
make Morgan's election sure, without revealing
to him any of his plans or information. The
result was, as the campaign progressed, Pop
saw less and less of the candidate, while the
boss saw more and more. The boss and Nutbourne became chums, they breakfasted together, they travelled the tenderloin together,
together they attended the pavers' balls. The

boss was master of the situation; he was preparing an appetizing feast for his revenge.
While professing his loyalty to the candidate,
the boss was in constant communication with
the nominee of the opposing convention, continually exposing to him the innermost plans
of the Morgan campaign, so that on election
day the strong man would be thwarted at every
point.   The boss was such a good, loyal, con-
sistent Republican!

Mulvenna had made his six speeches and
urged his hearers to vote for Mr. Morgan for
mayor.   And what was of more importance
than all, had received his *quid pro quo*. It was
the night before election day and he was
passing through the Parker House when he
was met by Nutbourne with the enquiry,

"Can I talk confidentially with you"?

To which the labor orator replied : —

"Did you ever have any difficulty in that
respect"?

"Now, Miles, you don't care about this
Morgan, do you? You've got your money.
Be with me.   Come down to Boston to-morrow
and tell those labor leaders to swing their
forces for the Democrat."

"What do I get out of it"? said Miles.

"I will see you have the naming of one of
the commissioners of public institutions.   You
ought to be able to make something out of
that."

" To — with this prairie boy Morgan! I'll do what you want, but how are you going to defeat him? Everybody seems to be for Morgan."

" Come, sit down here. I'll tell you."

These two politicians were a study. Under happier auspices, Mulvenna might have been admirable. He had wit, passion, a divine rage at injustice, an altogether companionable man, but the desire for money had warped each and every of these faculties and they had mortified. Not so with Nutbourne. Of him there was recorded no witty saying, no generous act, no loyal friendship, no heart of good fellowship— not a single attractive quality. I forget they did say he was a good family man. Nutbourne never had a friend he did not betray, or an enemy he did not slander. He never lifted a finger to help a friend unless he saw a money advantage to himself at the end of the act. Cold, calculating, continent, Corsican character, he made few speeches, uttered no jests, wrote nothing, cared naught for sports or entertainments, never was enticed by play, had no taste for art, painting, music, or statuary. He was ever well dressed, looked sleek as a croupier, and considered men but as pack horses who could carry him to the next relay of money. It goes without saying that he was energetic. When he displayed to his lieutenants the profits of his political steals, no one demurred. His adherents, with ecstatic glee, exclaimed, " What energy "!   And yet Nature, ever true to herself, had written "thief" on his countenance. That furtive glance, first to the right, then to the left, as though he were suspicious of the approach of a sheriff or police officer, stamped him as a transgressor.

While these two sat close together on a lounge in the hotel, a young porter edged his way towards them and caught every word.   It was Jimmie Hanks, him whom Pop had saved from the stern arm of the law.   Nutbourne, pleased to think he would have Mulvenna in his toils, fully revealed to him the plan he had devised for the defeat of Morgan,— plans that that very night Jimmie Hanks would lay before his benefactor.

" I shall work it this way," said the boss. " The returns will be held back in my strongholds, wards 13 and 19, until we learn what votes will be required to defeat Morgan.   Then the figures, made up at the moment, will be telephoned to headquarters.   The next day the city clerk, who has charge of the ballot boxes and is my warm friend, will alter the ballot boxes so as to correspond with the figures we send in the night before.   Do you think we can be beat "?

" No, I don't.   I 'll stir round to-morrow. Now I must get the train for Millville."

"Another gun spiked"! thought Nutbourne.

Mulvenna was feeling quite comfortable when he reached Millville and started on his long walk from the station to his home. In his trousers' pocket he carried the thousand dollars given him by Morgan for his labor addresses. In his mind he thought of the vacant commissionership he should have the right to fill by simply telling the walking delegates, the next day, to vote against Morgan. He had connected at both ends. Nothing like business!

Shortly after he left the station, he stopped at the new public library of Millville, which had recently been dedicated. In the old building there had been a fine oil painting of the original donor to the institution. But now all that was altered. In the space behind the librarian's desk he saw a full-length portrait of himself, on the frame of which was inscribed the words, "*A Man Incorruptible.*" As he read those words, think you his conscience smote him? Oh, no! Did not the money he had in his pocket burn at the very thought of the irony those words conveyed? Not much. Remorse exists only in the imagination of novelists and romancers. In reality it exists nowhere. Mulvenna never for a moment supposed his love for money and the means he employed for obtaining it were other than the exemplification of the command of the Bible "to be fervent in business." So he smiled at the picture and passed on to the narrow street that led to his very unpretentious abode. As he neared the house, he distinguished in the dark the presence of several people moving about the entrance.

"I wonder if it's some sort of a political surprise party," he queried, and bethought himself of what he should say if suddenly called upon to respond. But as he drew nearer, the faces of the people before him had a solemn look; there was shaking of heads, wringing of hands on the part of the women who had gathered about the gateway, and he thought he caught the sound of sighs and groans. An old friend stepped up to him as he approached the door, and placing his hand upon his shoulder in a fatherly way, said :

"I'm sorry for ye, my old friend, but cheer up. I do not think the worst we fear will happen. Be a man, Miles, as ye have always been. Your friends and neighbors are all with you in sympathy in this sad hour."

"Sad hour! Sympathy! What do you mean, man? Speak up. Why this crowd"? A thought flashed through his mind. "Has anything happened to my son Dick? Speak quick. Speak out. For God's sake spare this suspense. I must know."

"I am sorry to say, Miles, the boy is dead, and your wife——"

There was a wild cry. He brushed aside the friends that were gathering round him, hat off, and tearing his neck scarf as if he needed more air to breathe, with one bound he dashed up the flight of stairs that led to his chambers. At the door he was met by the calm and peaceful presence of the clergyman, whom he thrust aside, and with the laugh of a maniac, shouted : "Where's my boy, where's my wife? That boy for whom I toiled night and day, where is he? Give him to me, give him to me! My wife"? A faint groan from the bed showed that his partner had not long to live. Indistinctly he descried the presence of surgeons, of knives and instruments and blood. The smell of ether seemed to fill the room. No one dared to speak to him. He rushed across the entry way to the opposite chamber where, stretched on the lounge, cold and dead, lay the form of his only child, his idol, his hope, his life. And then, as if the whole world was against him, he pushed them all aside and grasped the surgeon's knife that lay upon the dresser. The strong arm of the priest stayed the act the agonized man was about to commit. Mulvenna waved his hands wildly in the air, stared vacantly about, uttered a piercing shriek, and threw himself upon the floor. When they raised him up a few seconds later, reason had fled, never to return this side of the grave.

That afternoon Mrs. Mulvenna and her son, while driving across one of the grade crossings in the suburbs which had been allowed to remain in a dangerous condition by Mulvenna having obtained, in consideration of a satisfactory fee from the railroad company whose tracks crossed the highway, an extension of the time necessary to elevate the roadbed, had been struck by the express flyer, and sustained the injuries which resulted in their death,—and destroyed the sanity of the dictator of Millville.

When the boss next morning read the account in the papers, he simply remarked:

"Who would think so hard-headed a man as Miles would allow himself to be carried away by such a trifling matter."

Morgan heard what had happened as he came down to breakfast, and sighed inwardly, with evident relief that further leg pulling in that direction was at an end.

Railroad officials and corporation directors expressed sympathy, while they congratulated themselves that one enemy was removed.

In Millville the whole population was bowed in heartfelt grief. The good father of his people, the "man incorruptible" would never protect them more. Who, now, would be their king!

Election day proved a veritable surprise to many. The day before all the papers prophesied the triumphant election of Morgan. But towards noon the bulletins put out by the press indicated a very close contest. Morgan's supporters were few in the very wards where a large vote had been claimed for him. The wards controlled by the boss, if anything could be judged by appearances about the polls, were going quite solidly for the opposing candidate.

Morgan, seated in his library, received from his various runners the earliest information from all parts of the city, and none of it was encouraging. Strange to say, the boss did not put in his appearance. For over ten days had he called every day at Morgan's residence, early in the morning. On this, of all days, he omitted his visit. It was one o'clock and no boss arrived. What was the cause? Morgan looked troubled. As advices kept coming to him, he saw that the vote that might finally defeat him would probably come from the boss' own wards.

"Can that man have proved treacherous to me"? he thought. As one after another of his adherents dropped in, he felt instinctively each brought worse news. And still where was his friend, Nutbourne? Perhaps Pop was right. Perhaps he had made a mistake in giving the boss his confidence. And then he went over in his mind the events of the past weeks. Re-called the story of his brother's crime, attempted to be laid at his door. Who could have started such a story, unless the boss? Who was more interested in having such a story circulated than the boss? Now, in the very hour of victory, the boss was to throw him down. And that, too, after his taking him into his confidence, and to him opening his pocket book? The pity of it! The pity of it! And he could say nothing. Whom should he dare to trust? They were all a pack of hungry hounds. All but Pop, and he had neglected him recently for the boss. Still, the agony would soon be over. It was nearing the hour when the polls would close, and Pop might be expected to call, in order to tabulate the returns. Still no word from the boss or his lieutenants and strikers. It was pretty evident the boss had played him for a "sucker," as it was called. Just as the hour struck which announced the closing of the polls, Pop rang the door bell. Morgan rushed to the door and opened it himself, eager to learn if Pop had any cheerful news for him. And in this he was not disappointed. The attorney had all the particulars from Jimmie Hanks as to the illegal course the boss intended to pursue, and his every action had been care-fully watched that day. The scheme was to declare Morgan defeated, send in improper returns at night and tinker the ballot boxes the next day so as to tally therewith. During the whole day the evidence against the boss had been multiplying, so Pop felt absolutely sure that if Morgan were defeated, he would on a fair recount be declared elected. He was, therefore, chipper, told his chief not to be worried about the vote as it came in on that night. He would guarantee him his subsequent election. But Morgan was doubtful. The strained expression that had been coming over his countenance ever since that sad night when the reporters queried him in reference to his past life, was now more marked. He had no hope as regards the result. He knew Pop was frank and true. But he himself was defeated. Said he felt it in his bones. Yes, he knew now the boss had betrayed him. And once more the reporters were ringing the door bell to see Mr. Morgan and get his views upon the result. All the returns received showed a fair lead for Morgan. But no word had been heard from Wards 13 and 19, the districts which the boss had agreed to deliver. These two wards were hopelessly Democratic and unless the boss carried out his promised and favorite program, of splitting that vote, Morgan would be defeated. The candidate looked at Pop in an apprehensive sort of a way.

"All this does n't trouble me," said that gentleman. "I know that eventually you will come out all right. No matter what my knowledge is now."

Morgan put his hand to the back of his head and complained of not feeling very well.

"You 'll feel all right to-morrow. I say you are elected."

"Elected"! Morgan had risen, as if in pain or confusion, looked enquiringly about, tried to stammer something, but it was with difficulty he could be understood. Made a mighty effort to finish the sentence, "Elected to what"? Then, his face growing purple, his eyes staring wildly, the foam coming to his lips, he reeled and fell to the floor with a sickening thud. They had given it to him in the neck. The boss was right. The boss always is right. The boss must be right. It is the law of nature, the survival of energy.

Cain had killed Abel. Cain always kills Abel. Cain *must* kill Abel. It is the divine law. Only so is there any progress. The material must triumph over the ideal, only through its death can the ideal live. There is no other explanation of the law of growth. Barrabas always is released, Christ always crucified. Why criticise? Why complain? Who would not infinitely prefer to be Cain alive than Abel dead, Barrabas free to

Christ crucified? Who desires the doubtful posthumous fame of a martyr, when he may have the glories of this world and be boss?

But the people! They who choose Cain rather than Abel! They who give freedom to Barrabas and death to Christ! They who spit upon honor and glorify the boss! What of *them!* Can all the corn and the cotton, can all the products of the foundry and loom, can all the triumphs of skill and art save them, so that in one jot or one tittle they can escape the fulfilment of the divine judgment that is ever decreed for those who prefer Cain to Abel, and Barrabas to Christ?